Odium 2.5

The Dead Saga
Origin Stories

By USA Today and
#1 Best-Selling British Horror Writer
Claire C. Riley

Also by Claire C. Riley

Odium 0.5 The Dead Saga
Odium I The Dead Saga.
Odium 1.5 The Dead Saga.
Odium II The Dead Saga.
Odium 2.5 The Dead Saga
Odium III The Dead Saga
Odium 3.5 The Dead Saga*
Odium VI The Dead Saga*
Limerence. (The Obsession Series)
Limerence II (The Obsession Series)
Limerence III (The Obsession Series)*
Twisted Magic Raven's Cover Series (Book One)

Short Stories/Anthology contributions
'Let's Scare Cancer to Death' anthology. **(Choices)**
Horror Novel Reviews Presents: One Hellacious Halloween
Volume One. **(The owl in the Tree)**
Fading Hope: Humanity Unbound anthology **(Honey-Bee)**
State of Horror Illinois anthology **(Out Come the Wolves)**
The Dark Carnival anthology **(Dancing Bear)**
At Hells Gates **(A Different Cocktail)**

Co-Authored Books

Thicker Than Blood #1
Beneath Blood and Bone #2
Shut Up & Kiss Me

Co-authored books written with USA Today Bestselling author
Madeline Sheehan

* Coming Soon

Dedication.

To zombie-loving book fans everywhere,
the end is nigh,
the apocalypse is upon us...

Remember to double-tap!

Odium 2.5

The Dead Saga
Origin Stories

By USA Today and
#1 Bestselling British Horror Writer
Claire C. Riley

HOUSE OF GLASS.
One.

Mathew.

The car behind bumps me forward in my seat as it slams into the back of mine. I laugh and curse all at the same time, turning to glare at who it is, thinking it's probably Daryl, my best friend from high school and now best friend in college.

I turn in my seat. "Hey, asshole, get a life, will you? We're on the same . . ." I let my words trail off as I stare into the eyes of the most beautiful girl I've ever seen.

Brown, shoulder-length hair, deep brown eyes, and a sprinkling of freckles across a little button nose. I take all this in within seconds, my brain taking a mental picture of her perfect face. The multi-colored lights flashing around us do nothing to stop my gaze. She giggles at my stare—honest to God giggles at me—and I can't hold back my nervous smile.

"Sorry, I thought you were my asshole friend," I yell over the noise.

She looks at me, her forehead crinkling in amusement as she tries to work out what I'm saying over the thumping techno music. I realize that both of us have stopped moving, our bumper cars at a standstill right in the center of the ring while we stare at each other like idiots. I catch movement from the corner of my eye before a red car slams into the right side of mine. The air leaves my lungs as another car hits the left side of mine, and my body slams sideways with an *umph*!

The girl giggles again, a hand covering her mouth in a gesture that's both sweet and sexy all at the same time. I turn and grin, ignoring the sound of Daryl's hyena-style laugh. The music still blasts far too loudly, the annoying lights continuing

1

to flash around us. And to think, I previously thought they were cool and retro; now I just find them annoying, and I want to get off this damn ride and away from all these distractions so I can talk to her.

I turn to Daryl as he backs up his car and rams me again, still hyena laughing. As he goes in for a third ram, the car stops and merely taps the side of mine as the ride finally comes to an end. He dives out and straight toward me with a huge grin, his bright orange hair flashing as it catches the multi-colored lights.

"Come on, dickface." He ruffles my hair and grabs the back of my T-shirt, still grinning as he practically lifts me out of my seat. At six-foot five and built like a college linebacker—because, well, he *is* a college linebacker—he outweighs me easily, but I'm no small guy either.

"Get off." I shrug out of his grip and turn to look at the girl.

But she's gone, and the weirdest thing happens: my heart skips a beat.

Daryl drags me from the bumper cars while he continues to chatter away. He heads toward the hotdog stand without even noticing my total distraction from what he's saying. We'd come to the fair with a couple of Daryl's football buddies—nice enough guys, if not a bit rowdy for my liking.

"Two chili dogs." He barks out the order to the bearded guy serving before turning to me. "'Sup with you, man? You got that goofy look on your face again."

My eyes scan the busy crowd of boisterous kids and irritated parents, looking for the girl from the bumper cars. "Nothing," I reply, still staring into the throng of people. "And what goofy look? I don't have a goofy look."

Daryl pushes me. "Sure you don't." He hands me my chili dog and we head off toward the funhouse. "Not like when

2

we were in high school and you'd go all gooey-eyed whenever Stacey Le'Hewitt walked into class. Oh shit, is that it?" He punches me in the arm.

"Is what it?" I dive away as he tries to tackle me.

"You've seen a girl?" He chuckles and takes a massive bite out of his food, not caring about what an asshole he's being.

"No," I snap, embarrassed at the mention of Stacey Le'Hewitt. That was a portion of my life I'd rather forget— though in a town this size, it's hard to do.

Stacey Le'Hewitt was just a girl, and I was just a boy. We were kids, but I thought it was true love. I know now that it wasn't—it was just two kids who liked each other an awful lot . . . only one moved on before the other. I've always believed in true love—the sort that you read about in books. Maybe that's because I was brought up by my mom—she used to read me Shakespeare every night—or maybe it's just in my DNA. Either way, it feels as if I've spent my entire nineteen years searching for The One. I look around me for the brown-eyed girl. Could she be it? It sure felt like nothing I've ever felt before.

The sun is beginning to set, casting a warm orange summer glow over the fairground and forming shadows around us. The air is thick with heat and alive with little bugs. The constant chirp of things can be heard from the small clumps of bushes and trees around the tents. I hate bugs. I swat at a little fly that gets too close to my face, feeling the humidity on my clammy skin.

We finish our chilidogs, scrunching up the wrappers as we arrive at the funhouse, and both of us drop them to the ground, throw a dollar each to the bored-looking vendor of the ride, and head inside. It's dark and stuffy, the bad fluorescent paint job on the crappy plywood walls showing the age of this thing. We balance over wobbly floors and make dumb faces in the crazy mirrors before heading back out the other side of the ride.

"That was a bust. Wanna to go back to the bumper cars?" Daryl asks.

It's a little darker than when we went in, but not by much. However, strings of cheap lights have been turned on around the fairground. I scan the crowd for *her* again, but continue to come up short.

"Sure, if you want." I shrug noncommittally and look down as I stuff my hands into my jeans pockets.

We head back over to the bumper cars, kicking a couple of stray cans that people have dropped on the way and chatting about the summer so far. Daryl has been struggling with the extra workload of college, and his mom is making him get a tutor when we go back after the break so he doesn't fall too far behind. I haven't found it that bad, though I've had more of a social life than I normally like. I'm not a great one for meeting new people, but between Daryl's boisterous nature and what he calls my "boyish good looks," it's been difficult to try and blend into the background like I prefer to do.

I stare at my white sneakers as we walk, burping out my chili dog and regretting eating it as the taste is regurgitated back into my mouth unpleasantly. Daryl continues to chatter away again, once more unaware of me only paying half as much attention as I should be. It's always been like this with us—probably why we've been friends for so long. He is the fast-talking joker and I'm the quiet one. We complement each other perfectly without cramping each other's style.

"Did you see that? There's a fight." Daryl tugs on my T-shirt and I look up.

Sure enough, he's right: a fight's broken out between a couple of dudes. By the looks of the girls bitching at each other to the side of them, I'd say they were probably the cause. Parents are dragging their little kids away from the fight—not only because of the violence, but because of the cuss words flying around. The whole thing makes me groan and roll my eyes.

A crowd closes around the two guys fighting and I follow Daryl over as he laughs and whoops manically. Me, I'm a lover not a fighter, and the sound of fists hitting flesh makes my stomach churn. It's not that I can't fight, it's that I choose not to—not unless I have to. And when I do it's usually to back up Daryl, since he seems to attract trouble wherever he goes. I follow him into the throng of people, pushing aside a couple that with a polite "excuse me." I get some shifty stares but most people are too preoccupied with watching these guys beating on each other to really care. The shrill voices of the girls arguing close by echo throughout the crowd, and I'm pretty certain that it's only moments now before those two start pulling at each other's hair like only girls can do.

I finally push to the front and see that a dark-haired guy has a smaller blond-haired guy pinned to the ground as he lays into him, his fists repeatedly flying into the guy's face as the blond guy snarls up at him.

Daryl is still laughing and egging them on much like everyone else, but it does nothing for me in any way. The sight and smell of the blood is just gross, and I can't quite grasp what enjoyment people can get from watching this. I turn to head back out of the crowd and bump straight into Brown Eyes.

Two.

"You again." She smiles as she says it, letting me know that she's being playful. "What's happening there?" She points behind me.

I shrug and smile back to her. "Couple of jocks beating on each other, nothing new." I try to act casual—nonchalant, almost.

"Ugh, jocks." She chuckles.

Behind us the girls are screaming at each other, and I'm guessing that means that they've started their little bitch fight.

"Do you wanna, umm, go somewhere…less noisy?" I ask shyly.

"Less violent?" she adds on and takes my hand.

She turns and pulls us through the crowd. Her hand in mine is warm, her skin soft, whereas mine feels clammy…and growing more so with each second that she holds my hand in hers, but I don't want to let it go.

We escape from the crowd and she continues to hold my hand as she pulls me toward the clay pigeon shooting. She glances back over her shoulder and smiles, and I see a small blush creep up her neck and cheeks. We come to a stop at the stall laden with colorful teddy bears hanging from hooks.

"Three tries for five dollars," the bored vendor says, holding out the long-barreled gun to me. He's a scruffy middle-aged guy who looks like he's been drinking away his life.

I turn to Brown Eyes. "You want a teddy bear?"

She nods happily and my heart skips again.

"Yes, please. If you think you can. I mean, these things are rigged, right?" She pays no mind to the scowling vendor.

I look at her: she's much shorter than I—probably only five feet, three inches, even in her little heels; her hair looks soft to the touch, and I know her skin is. Everything about her seems delicate and precious.

"If you want a teddy bear, I'll get you a teddy bear," I say confidently and hand the vendor my five dollars, shooting him a cocky grin.

I take aim with the gun, staring down the barrel of it and noticing that it's off by a millimeter or so. That'll put a slight curve on the pellet and make it almost impossible to win. Almost.

I readjust my aim, taking into account the curve, and pull the trigger, hitting the clear glass bottles at the back of the stall dead center and knocking the top three over. Two more shots and the tower of nine bottles have fallen. I feel victorious as Brown Eyes cheers and hugs me. Her arms feel *right* around me. You know the way ketchup goes with a burger and the salt goes on fries. We feel like two things that just *belong* together. She must feel it too, because she pulls back a little, her cheeks flushed as she looks up at me and smiles.

"Which one did you want?" I say and gesture to all the dangling teddies.

She picks out a pink one with a red bow around its neck and the vendor grudgingly hands it over. Brown Eyes slips her hand in mine and we walk away.

"How did you do that?" she asks, a small skip in her step. "Do you often shoot guns?" She chuckles.

I laugh back. "Me and my uncle go hunting all the time," I say and smile at her sideways.

"Wow," she says. "You're really good."

"I'm better with a bow. But if I'm being really honest, I don't like shooting things. I'd much rather pet a deer than kill it." I cringe, thinking I sound like a total asshat, but she doesn't say anything and when I chance a glance at her, she's still smiling and staring at her feet.

The music from the fairground is quieter as we move away from the main part and toward the Ferris wheel. The strings of lights shine around us, making her hair shine and her eyes sparkle. The poet in me is already imagining what it would feel like to kiss her soft pink mouth and run my fingers through her silky tresses.

"Two, please," I say to the vendor and look at Brown Eyes, making sure she's okay with me taking the lead.

She nods, and we climb into the little seat and I pull the bar down over us, and slowly the ride begins to lift. The cart swivels on its hinges as we get higher, the air cooler up here yet still humid with the summer heat. We have a great view over the entire fairground up here, and for a moment I'm lost within the moment of the feel of her body next to mine and the lights dancing down below.

"It's so pretty," she says.

I turn in my seat to look at her. "I was thinking the same thing," I say bashfully.

She starts to say something and then stops and looks away. When she looks back at me, her cheeks are flushed again. "This is weird, right? I mean, it's perfect and weird, and…"

"Can I kiss you?" I say without thinking. Jesus, where did that come from? She doesn't even know me, and I'm asking to kiss her. I brace myself for a slap across the face, but she only nods lightly, the blush creeping further up her cheeks.

I lean in, my hands holding onto the sides of her face, her hair soft on my fingers. I press my mouth against hers and her lips part for me, and then our tongues are dancing against one another and she steals my breath away.

8

I pull out of our kiss and stare into her eyes, and I know that Brown Eyes feels it too: this is love at first sight.

Three.

"So, you do this with all the girls you first meet, huh?" Brown Eyes laughs.

I clasp her hand tightly in mine as we go back around the Ferris wheel for the sixth or seventh time. I gave the vendor twenty bucks in the end to let us just stay on for as long as we wanted. I can't afford it, really. I only work part-time at a bakery, but I'm hoping to get into something with computers once I finish college.

"This," I gesture to our entwined hands, "or this?" I lean over and kiss her again.

"Both." She laughs, kissing me back.

"Nah, I actually just came out of a horrible relationship," I say.

Her brow puckers.

"I'm sorry, I don't know why I told you that. You didn't need to know," I say hurriedly.

"It's okay, I want to know all about you," she says and then looks down to her feet shyly.

The sky has darkened, the sun finally set, and the moon has risen high in the sky. It's a clear night, with stars shining over the entire fairground.

"It's lovely up here, don't you think?" Brown Eyes doesn't look at me as she says this.

"It sure is," I say contentedly, still staring at the side of her face.

The wheel gets lower to the ground again, and I finally see Daryl with our friends looking around for me. He catches my eye, and cheers as our little cart goes back up.

"You know those guys?" Brown Eyes asks with a quirk of her eyebrow, watching Daryl make an idiot of himself as he does a goofy dance.

I shrug apologetically. "Unfortunately so."

Flashing lights in the distance distract me from the rest of my sentence, and I see two or three police cars screeching into the fairground. I frown as a couple of the officers jump out and start shouting at people, pointing at them and shoving them to one side. One officer grabs a megaphone and starts yelling into it, but as the ride goes higher, his words are muffled out.

"What do you think is going on?" Brown Eyes asks curiously.

I shrug. "I have no idea." I watch Daryl head over to the police, and I feel happy that he'll handle the situation and come back to let me know what's going on. "I'm sure it's nothing," I say quietly.

One of the officers fires a gun into the crowd and everyone starts screaming and backing away—all but one. Brown Eyes squeezes my hand tighter and yelps as another shot sounds out from somewhere. I scan the area, trying to pinpoint where the gunshot came from. It doesn't sound like the pellet gun I shot earlier, but a real gun. The ride is close to the ground again now, and I can see that the vendor has left his station—obviously gone to see what's happening with the police; or hell, maybe he's run away and is hiding somewhere. That seems like the smartest move, despite my current predicament of being stuck on his damn ride with no way off. I look around at the other people that are on the Ferris wheel, noticing that they look just as worried as we are.

"That doesn't sound like nothing," she whispers.

I can't help but think that she's right as another shot rings out louder, sounding closer to us, and I watch more people scream and run away, scattering like mice in every direction. One of the police officers steps in front of someone and fires his gun twice more, and further screaming ensues. I can't stop myself from flinching at the sound—and the image, even from this distance. Brown Eyes grabs onto my elbow and I hear her gasp, but I'm so lost in what is happening that I barely acknowledge it.

Another man steps toward the officer, lurching forward, and as he moves I see a body on the ground, with a dark patch of something that I can only assume is blood surrounding it. The sky is getting darker now, and it's making it harder to see from this distance. The Ferris wheel continues to turn, sending us back up into the night sky, and in some ways I'm grateful for the separation from the chaos, but in others, I want to get off this thing and find out what the hell is happening.

"We need to get off," Brown Eyes says, pulling my face to hers as she searches my features for some form of answer.

I nod, but she doesn't see it, her eyes moving off to stare at the police cars and the fuss surrounding them. Most people have scattered to a safe distance, but some people look like they are trying to help. I can't make out exactly what is happening, but I can tell that the situation is getting out of hand. I look for Daryl and see him fighting with another guy, and I groan and shake my head.

"What's wrong?"

"I need to go help my friend," I say and point to Daryl with a frown. He's going to get into some serious shit if he gets caught fighting again. "What about your friends? Who did you come with?" I turn in my seat to see her more clearly.

"I came with my mom and dad, but they've already left. I told them I was going to stick around for a little longer." Her eyes are wide with worry and my gut clenches, knowing that she stayed so that she could look for me. If anything happens to her, it will be my fault.

The wheel goes back toward the ground, and I think about jumping off. The vendor hasn't come back yet, and instead we're all forced to endure another ride around the wheel, which suddenly doesn't feel quite so romantic anymore.

There are a couple of people staggering around, and before the ride gets too high I shout down to one of them. "Hey, mister, can you turn this thing off please?"

An older man with graying hair and a moustache looks over to us and I gasp loudly as I see his face: blood covers the front of his shirt and his lips peel back to reveal a bloodied mouth. He snarls and lurches toward us.

"Oh shit," I mutter. I follow with my eyes as our car goes higher up. "What's wrong with you?"

He stumbles on the small steps as he tries to get up to the ride, and as he makes it up to the platform I think he's going to work the controls for it and help get us off, right before he turns away from the control board and reaches for a car with a woman and child in it. They scream and kick out as he grabs at their legs, and as the ride lifts higher, he clings onto them.

Four.

The mother and child continue to scream loudly, the mother saying more curse words than she probably ever thought she would in front of her daughter. The kid can't be more than nine years old, with long blond hair tied into pigtails. She's small and manages to pull her legs all the way up into the car so they aren't dangling down anymore, but the mother can't, and the man continues to grab onto her leg, despite how much she shakes and kicks to get him off it. Her scream hitches up a notch as he buries his face into her ankle and pulls his head back, bringing her clothing away with him.

I gasp as he burrows his face into her leg again. This time an arc of blood sprays out from the wound, and when he pulls back he's chewing, and fresh blood covers his face. The mother begins to scream loudly, her legs frantically kicking out.

The little girl cries loudly and looks around her before she grabs for the mother's black handbag. She reaches over the side and swings the bag at the man. He barely flinches and she swings back again. It hits the side of his head, but again he doesn't seem to notice and continues to pull flesh from her mother's leg. The little girl drops her legs down and kicks at him hard until one of his hands comes loose from its grip, and he dangles with only one hand.

Realization hits me in the gut, and even though it shouldn't matter—I shouldn't care because of what he's doing—I can't stop my automatic reaction as I yell, "Wait."

The little girl stands back up and swings with the bag again as her mother screams in agony.

"Stop, he'll fall!" I yell louder, knowing I'm being ridiculous—knowing that I should be glad he'll fall and most likely die. He's literally eating that woman alive, but instincts are just that: instincts—and you can't stop your automatic reaction to something. I try to stand up again as our car reaches the peak of the circle, but the bar holds me in place, allowing only a little movement. "Stop!" I holler.

The woman pays me no attention, too trapped within her own pain, but the little girl hears me and looks up at me. Her eyes meet mine and I see pure fear written across her face right before the ride comes to a jittering halt and she slips over the side and falls to the ground with an ear-piercing scream. She hits the ground below with a heavy thump and her screams stop right away. A shudder runs through me as I watch blood seep around her and soak the ground.

Brown Eyes gasps next to me, her hand releasing from mine as she clasps it over her mouth. I try again to stand in my seat, but still get no closer to freedom. The mother is screaming incessantly—from the fact that her daughter just plunged to her death or because of the man currently biting into her ankle, I'm not sure.

"I want to get off now, I want to get off," Brown Eyes sobs repeatedly.

I look down to the lifeless body of the little girl. It's raining blood on top of her from her mother's leg wound as the man continues to bite down on her, *growling, chewing, growling, chewing.* The mother is still screaming endlessly, and I have no idea what to do. I look at the other people on the ride and then to Brown Eyes, but she refuses to look at me.

The ride suddenly shudders and starts again, knocking the man loose from the woman. He falls through the sky and lands right on top of the little girl's dead body, and everyone around us stops screaming, stops moving, and stares. The man then does the strangest thing: after a moment of stillness, he flips himself slowly around and begins to gorge on the body of the girl.

The mother screams again and Brown Eyes sobs louder, and all I can do is stare in total horror. As our cart gets back to the ground and the other cars move higher up, the ride comes to a stop again and I feel the pitter-patter of something on my shoulder. I touch it with my hand and stare at my fingers when they come away red. Brown Eyes screams next to me and shuffles in her seat to get away from me, but there's no avoiding the blood that pours down on us from the injured woman. Her cart is at the peak now of the ride now, and showering everyone else on the Ferris wheel with her blood.

I look at the controls and see Daryl standing there, a large two-by-four in his hands, as the man that's gorging on the girl looks up at him and growls. We're low down, almost at the platform, and it makes the growl seem louder and more out of place in the fairground, where only ten minutes ago people were screaming and yelling with happiness, and now… now people are running and screaming for their lives.

Daryl chances a glance at me, and I can see the blood covering the front of his sweatshirt and hands.

"What are you waiting for—an invitation? Get off," he yells to me.

I push at the bar but it still won't budge. I shake it as violently as possible, creating a clanging noise of metal on metal. The injured man looks across to me. Brown Eyes screams in fear as he climbs back up to his feet and lunges for us.

"The button, hit the release button," I yell to Daryl, but it comes out more of a strangled scream as the man gets closer, slipping up the small step to the ride and falling over. His jaw hits the ground hard, and even over the noise—the screaming, the music, the gunshots that have erupted around us like the Fourth of July—even with all of that, I hear a loud *crack* as his jaw slams against the metal.

It doesn't faze him, though: he looks up undeterred, his jaw swinging loosely, and begins to stand back up with a throaty snarl. As his mouth opens wide, Brown Eyes gets a full view of the inside, seeing his shattered and bloodied teeth, and begins to scream louder, struggling to pull herself free from the car.

"The release button, asshole!" I yell at Daryl again.

Instead of hitting the release button, Daryl swings at the man's head with the two-by-four, slamming it into the side of his skull with a loud *thwack.* The man starts to turn, his arms still reaching for us even as his mouth is snapping at Daryl. But with a second crack of wood upon bone, the man falls down, his body twitching every now and then but thankfully not getting back up. Thankfully? Daryl just killed someone—how can I be thankful for that. As the blood rain continues to drench us, I realize exactly how.

Daryl finally hits the release button and our bar makes a small *clink* sound to show that it is open. Brown Eyes is out and running before I can tell her to wait. Lucky for me, Daryl grabs her around the waist and stops her from running off too far. She screams and hits out at him, but he continues to hold her.

I climb out on shaky legs, cautiously stepping over the still-twitching body of the man and the crushed body of the little girl, and take over from Daryl, letting Brown Eyes cling to me while she sobs. Daryl moves the cars down one by one, releasing everyone until we get to the mother of the little girl. Everyone runs as soon as they get off, but her—she stays seated, her eyes never leaving her daughter. Brown Eyes pushes away from me and steps toward the woman, offering out her hand. The woman takes it and hops out of the car, stumbling on her damaged leg as she puts an arm around Brown Eyes and hops over to her little girl.

"Call an ambulance," Brown Eyes says softly to me.

"Emma?" she whispers, and I cringe.

When the little girl had no name, it didn't seem as real, but she's Emma now: a little girl with blond pigtails who loved the Ferris wheel and tried to save her mom. Now she's dead, and this shit is real.

"We need to go, man." Daryl tugs on my elbow.

I pull out my phone and look at him, swallowing back horror and fear. "The girl," I say quietly. "She needs an ambulance."

Daryl looks around us with a shrug. "It's Armageddon, man, no one's answering that anytime soon." He nods toward my phone and then looks around us.

Everywhere has gone quiet, apart from the music blaring from each ride. You would think it was just a real quiet night at the fair, but looking closer, that's not true. Blood smears several of the tents that house attractions, bodies lie prone on the ground. The police cars lights still flash, illuminating several bodies close by them.

I look back at Brown Eyes and the woman with Emma. I watch the woman gently push the hair back from Emma's face to reveal purple bruising, and blood seeping from her nose and eyes—the same eyes that stare up at nothing. The woman cries louder and Brown Eyes looks to me to do something, but there's nothing I can do. Emma is dead, and it's partly my fault. If I hadn't shouted at her to stop, maybe she never would have fallen.

The woman looks pale and shaky, tears free-flowing down her cheeks. Blood has pooled around her from her injured leg, and I take a moment to really look at how bad it is and wince. The man has bitten right through her thin tights and into the fleshy part of her calf muscle. I'm almost certain that I can see bone, and I gulp and look back at Daryl. He's picked up his two-by-four again and is looking around us anxiously.

I step forward to get Brown Eyes to come with us and realize that I don't actually know her name. If I could hashtag this, I would: #awkward. I'm about to reach out and touch her shoulder when I hear someone close by.

"We gotta go, Matty," Daryl says behind me. His voice sounds strong, yet I can hear the slight quaver to it.

"What's going on?" Brown Eyes looks up at me from her place next to the woman, blood from the bodies pooling around her knees. "Why would that guy do this? Where are the police?" She looks from me to Daryl and back again before slowly standing and looking around us. "What's wrong with everyone?" Her voice sounds desperate, like she's begging me to answer her, to give her the answers that she needs.

Her face holds the same expression I presume mine did several seconds ago as she begins to notice the lack of people and the blood everywhere. When her eyes come back to meet mine there's a determination there.

"I need to get home to my parents," she says and stands. She looks down at the woman. "I'm sorry. We'll bring back help, I promise." She walks away without a second glance.

I stare after her in amazement, admiring her strength of character but confused as to how she could just turn it all off like that. Daryl casts a look back at the woman, who's still crying over the body of her child, before following me. There's nothing we can do for her now but go get help—if there's any help left to find.

Five.

It's a funny thing when you see the world in a different light. When we arrived I thought this place was pretty cool: tons of rides, food stalls, flashing lights and loud music, the smell of popcorn and cotton candy filling my nose. Now, the whole place seems like a walking nightmare. And instead of the sweet smell of cotton candy, I smell blood and decay.

"You good, man?" Daryl steps to my side, and Brown Eyes gives us both a quick nervous glance.

"Yeah," I reply. "Why?"

Daryl frowns, his eyes looking me over. "The blood." He gestures at me, his hand still clutching his two-by-four.

I look down at myself, seeing blood splattered down my jeans and across my T-shirt. I suck in a breath, feeling a mixture of things, but mainly feeling dirty. I look at Brown Eyes and see that she's in the same predicament as me, though I wonder if she knows.

"I'm, I'm fine. It's not mine." I look into the shadows between two stalls; nothing jumps out, so we quickly move forward. "What's going on, Daryl?"

"No clue, man. People just started going crazy after that fight. The police turned up and tried to separate them. They had someone in the back of their car, and he just started going mental. After that, I don't know. Everyone was either running or fighting."

As we pass the shooting stall, I realize how unarmed I am. Daryl has his shitty piece of wood, but I've got nothing. "I need to be armed. I need…I dunno, something."

Daryl grabs me by the shoulder and pulls me to a stop. He nods to the pellet guns on the rack—the ones I had earlier used to win Brown Eyes her pink teddy. I shrug: a pellet gun is better than nothing, I guess, and if nothing else I can smack someone with it.

"Hey?" I whisper to Brown Eyes.

She stops and looks back at me, her eyes wide and frightened but her jaw strong and determined.

"Let me grab a gun."

Her eyes go even wider upon hearing my words, but she nods an *okay* and I climb up onto the stand and jump down the other side before she can say anything else. There are lots of guns, but they're all chained to the stand, so I rummage around underneath the counter to try and find a spare but still come up blank. When I stand back up, Daryl and Brown Eyes are nowhere to be seen.

"Daryl?" I whisper-shout. I lean over the stall and look around. I can see someone in the distance, but nothing and no one close by. "Daryl?" I shout-whisper again, my words dying out as the fairground music stops abruptly. Seconds later the lights go out and the entire fairground is plunged into darkness.

"Shit," I whisper.

I look around, my eyes slowly adjusting to the darkness, my senses becoming more aware of everything and nothing all at the same time. The only lights are the ones still coming from the top of the patrol car, which continue to flash on and off as if the fair is still going.

A growl to my left makes me pull my head back inside the stall, and before I even know I'm doing it, I crouch down under the counter, blending my body into the darker shadows. Minutes go by before I hear someone—or something—getting closer, and I nearly stand up to see if it's Daryl. It's the smell that hits me first and makes me know it isn't him. Sure, the guy has been known to stink on occasion—doesn't every guy?— but this is unlike anything I've ever smelled before. I gag on the taste of it in my mouth, the smell making me retch. I shake my head to clear the stench from my nose, and try to man up to it all, a grimace covering my face as I thankfully hear the steps receding.

I wait another minute before slowly extracting myself from my hiding position, peeking up over the top of the stall. It's gotten even darker, but thankfully the police lights are illuminating enough for me to see that my way is clear. It also shows me that on the other side of the fair is another shooting stand, but this one is bows and arrows. I don't know where Daryl and Brown Eyes have gone, but I need to get one of those bows and some arrows, no matter how cheap they seem: it's better than nothing, and I'm a damn good shot with an arrow.

I stand fully up, preparing to climb back over the stall and head over to grab my bounty, but my foot slips on one of the metal chains holding the crappy guns to the table and I trip, grabbing the table behind me for balance. I breathe a sigh of relief just in time for nine glass bottles to clatter and fall from their stand. I wince and pray that the sound just seems incredibly loud to me, but when a low chorus of moans and growls echoes around the fairground, I know I don't have much time.

I dive over the stall and run as fast as I can, my sneakers digging into the hard summer ground and sending up dust behind me. I leave behind the sound of moans and the clatter of bottles and cheap guns falling and grit my teeth as I push harder and faster to get to the bows and arrows. Shadows move around me, and as I focus on one, more appear. My stomach lurches of its own accord, giving me the impression that now would be a perfectly normal time to freak the hell out—if not wholly inconvenient. The thought of Brown Eyes and my best friend needing my help keeps me strong and moving forward, toward my weapon.

I reach the stall, place one hand on top, and throw myself over the other side of it. I shoulder slam into the ground and try to stop my momentum from knocking over the stand and causing too much more noise. I can hear growls coming from all around me, and I try to slow my breathing and make it as quiet as possible, hiding under the stall—almost mimicking my previous position.

Reaching my hand around the ground, I feel numerous bows and I carefully pull one to me. It feels good in my hand— strong—even though I know it's probably made of cheap wood. I know it will fire if I need it to. With my other hand, I root across the dark ground, feeling for arrows, finding several in a box. The points are pretty blunt, but hopefully with enough power behind them they can still do some good.

I look around me in the darkness for something I can use to carry the arrows, but it's too dark, and I don't dare get my iPhone out to use the built-in flashlight. I shuffle out from under the stall when my breathing has returned to normal and I don't hear any movement close by. The cop car's blue light reflects off the back of the stall, and I can see a small brown backpack, which would be perfect to carry the arrows, hanging near a coat.

I peek over the top of the stall, my blood freezing in my veins when I see a dark shadow lurch from around the police car. In the flash of blue it's clear that this man is missing most of his face. I gasp involuntarily and he pauses mid-lurch, lifting his nose in the air before finally turning in my direction with a low growl.

"Shit," I mumble. I glance back at the bag, knowing that if I stand up and make a grab for it, I'll be giving away my position. But what choice do I have? I can't carry around a handful of arrows, and I need to find Daryl and Brown Eyes quickly.

A long, piercing scream makes up my mind and I abruptly stand and grab the backpack off the hook. It snags on something on the wall, and for a few precious seconds I don't think it's going to come free. When it does, I'm pulling so hard that I collapse backwards into the stand and knock a ton of things over. The faceless man growls louder, his growl joined by several more, each echoing around me. I grab handfuls of arrows and thrust them into the bag before throwing it over my shoulders and sliding it onto my back as I start to run.

The faceless man is nearly upon me by the time I climb over the other side.

But I'm not worried about him anymore.

I'm worried about the other ten or so monsters that have come out from wherever they were hiding—each one a new horror to see.

Another long, piercing scream sounds out, and I throw caution to the wind and run in the direction of it, dodging reaching arms and bodies that try to stop me as rotten smells invade my senses and make my eyes water.

I run, passing several dead bodies that litter the ground that I try not to look at too closely, past blood-smeared stalls and overturned food carts, until I come to the House of Glass— the place the screaming is coming from.

Six.

Bodies surround the place, both dead and alive—well, sort of alive—and I'm about to go in search of my friends somewhere else when I hear Daryl's loud ass shouting. Another scream and I'm almost certain that they are both inside the House of Glass. A noise behind me makes me turn just in time to see long, gangly arms reaching for me, and I duck and run to the entrance.

I slam into the doorway, skidding to a halt as my eyes adjust to the dimness inside. I take a breath and try to ignore the pounding of my brain as a migraine begins to throb behind my eyes. My hand still clutches onto the bow, but in here it won't be any good: there's not enough space to be able to shoot it properly. I pull an arrow out of the backpack, feeling the point and knowing it's not really sharp enough for what I want—not unless I put a helluva lot of strength behind it. Passing the bow over my shoulder, I travel further inside.

I can hear Daryl shouting and Brown Eyes sobbing, but I don't immediately find them. Instead, I'm forced to travel through the maze of glass walls. Things eventually go quiet. It's dark and confusing as hell in here. Every now and then I bump into a glass wall, my face slamming into the warm sheet of glass that I thought was a doorway.

I try not to panic, putting every thought I have into finding Daryl, because wherever he is, I know he'll have Brown Eyes and I know he'll look after her for me. I bump into the wall again, and curse under my breath. A bloody hand slams onto the other side of the glass, a face appearing seconds later.

The face is unlike anything I've ever seen before—bloody, with chunks of nose missing—and for a minute all I can do is stare. The face—the man—snaps at me, his teeth trying to bite through the glass. I gulp, knowing what I'm seeing but not quite believing it because up close this is even more horrifying. It head-butts the glass and growls, and I hit the other side—partly in anger, partly in fear. It—he—doesn't care, though; he head-butts again and again until the skin on his forehead splits and blood seeps out. Every time he slams his head against it, fresh blood splatters onto the glass.

I take a step back, feeling intensely claustrophobic—and yeah, wanting to get away from the freak cracking his skull open in front of me. I reach out and fumble my way around another confusing glass corner, seeing movement once more on the other side of the glass, but this time the movements aren't jerky and freakish, this time I can see that it's Daryl: his orange hair is like a beacon to me even in the dimness.

I bang on the glass and yell to get his attention. He's facing the opposite way, and is walking backwards. I bang again and he glances over his shoulder toward me, his eyes going wide when he sees me. In his arms is Brown Eyes, and in front of them another one of the freaks with a gaping wound in its neck.

"Matty!" Daryl shouts to me, the panic evident in his voice.

"Daryl," I yell back, and feel my way along the walls to try to get to them, but with every corner turned, I seem to be getting further away from them. Panic courses through me and I shout in frustration.

I can hear her crying loudly. I can hear the growls of the . . . people, and I can hear Daryl yelling for me to help, but I can't damn well find my way to them. I slam a hand against the glass, imitating the freak from earlier. I turn on my heel and continue to scramble around in the glass maze, every once in a while the stench of rot filling my nostrils and making me turn in a different direction.

I turn a corner and my foot slips in something on the ground. I stop but don't look down, knowing what it is but not wanting the clarification of it.

"Daryl?" I whisper hoarsely, still not wanting to look down.

No voice comes back to me, so I say it again, quieter this time. "Daryl? Brown Eyes?" I squeeze my eyes shut, take a breath, and reluctantly look down to my feet.

Brown Eyes stares back up at me, her complexion paler than snow, and her lips have a blue tinge to them. Blood bubbles sluggishly out of a hole in her neck, and for a second I think she's okay, that she's not really…dead. But when I look at the rest of her body, I see the real horror: an empty cavity where her stomach once was, her intestines trailing out of her like worms exploding from a can.

I squeeze my eyes shut against the image, only opening them when I hear a shuffling sound. I grip the arrow in my hand tighter, ready to slam it into the body of whatever comes at me. Daryl comes around the corner, his hair matted to his head, his movements awkward, and his stare vacant. He growls at me, baring bloody teeth and wrenching a sob from my chest.

"Daryl, man, what the hell happened to you?" I don't know why I ask—I know he won't answer. But I do.

He cocks his head to one side in an animalistic gesture and reaches for me. I drag a hand down my face, wiping away silent tears and sweat. He trips on Brown Eyes's body, stumbling into me, mouth snapping, and I catch him, holding him at arm's length. He fights against me, the scent of death thick on him.

"Daryl, man, I love you." I reach back and slam the arrow tip into the side of his head just as his face gets too close to mine. He stops immediately as I feel the arrow pierce his skull and embed in his brain.

He collapses against me, and this time I cradle his dead body against mine, sliding down to the floor and sitting amongst the blood and body parts.

Seven.

I don't know how long I sit there, but the blood has begun to dry on my clothes by the time I decide to stand back up. I check my phone after laying Daryl down carefully next to Brown Eyes. I kiss her cold lips and close her eyelids for her, and say goodbye to them both.

There's no signal on my phone, not even a busy signal, and strangely as I stumble around and find myself back outside, the outside seems much calmer than when I went in. I peer around carefully, checking for the...people, but seeing and hearing nothing.

I walk silently, sticking to the shadows and away from the dead bodies that still litter the ground. My mind fumbles with what to do and where to go. I traipse without intention, coming to a stop as I lean against the side of a stall to get my bearings on everything that has happened. I realize that I'm standing by the popcorn stand, and I reach in without even thinking and grab a handful and fill my mouth.

The saltiness is refreshing after the bitter taste of bile and rot that has filled it for the last couple of hours, and strangely it settles my anxious stomach. I grab another handful, thinking through a plan that could be either genius or stupid—because it seems obvious to me now what this is.

Daryl had it both right and wrong when he said this was Armageddon: this is a zombie apocalypse. These aren't people—not anymore. They're the dead, and they're walking around again. Without my best friend, and Brown Eyes, nothing seems important anymore, apart from killing as many of these things as possible and putting an end to this and their misery before it destroys any more lives.

29

I rub my hand down my pants and grab one of the cans of soda from the stand, not bothering to leave a dollar for it since no one is there to accept. I swallow the entire thing down and grab another, all the time my eyes and ears and watching and listening for movement. I throw a couple of the cans into my backpack for later and set off for the army base in the mountains. My uncle used to tell me about it when he looked after me while Mom worked her night shifts. I'm grateful that neither of them are alive to see all of this happening now.

As I pass the entrance, the large fairground sign overhead swinging in the light evening breeze, I hear soft crying coming from between the parked cars. My hand clutches my bow tighter and I move toward it. My head screams at me to go in the opposite direction, but my heart tells me that I have to do the right thing; I have to try to save people if I can. That's how I was brought up—to be a man and help others that can't defend themselves. I'm a lover, not a fighter—but I can be a fighter if I need to be. And right now that's who and what I need to be.

I edge toward the sound of crying, my heart pummeling the inside of my chest. I crouch next to the front of a car, count to three, and peer around it. A woman with curly hair gives a short, sharp scream before scrambling backwards and falling on her ass.

"Please don't, please," she begs loudly.

"Shhh," I whisper angrily, aware of the noise she's making.

"Please, please!" she says again, continuing to scramble away.

"Lady, shush, please," I say louder to try to get her to calm down.

A figure appears from behind her, and for a second I think it's another survivor. For a second I'm glad to have someone to help me calm this crazy woman down—that is until the figure steps forward and growls.

The woman screams loudly, unsure which direction to go in now, since both of her exits appear to be blocked.

"Aah, crap." I stand up and take aim with my bow. As the zombie steps forward and I make a hundred percent certain that it is in fact a zombie and not another survivor, I release my arrow and hit it between the eyes.

It sticks into its forehead, but doesn't go deep enough to stop it in its tracks, so I grab another arrow and fire again. This one embeds itself into its head, and it pauses in its lurching before hitting the ground like a sack of potatoes.

The woman screams again, her hands covering her face.

"Shut up! You're going to bring every one of these things to us," I shout-whisper.

The woman stops screaming but continues to sob. She clamps a shaky hand across her mouth, but doesn't move to stand up. I reach down and pull my arrows from the zombie's head, not relishing in the sensations of them tugging on the skull as I wrench it free. I shake off the excess blood with a grimace, my stomach feeling queasy as the stench rises and fills my nose. The woman gags and I look across to her.

"Are you okay?" I ask.

She stares at me, her eyes wide. "What's happening?" Her chin trembles.

"I don't really know." I hold out a hand. She takes it and I pull her to her feet. Taking a look around us to make sure no more are on their way, I reply. "But I think it's the apocalypse."

She snorts out a dry laugh. "Don't…don't be stupid." She says it, but by the look of fear on her face it's obvious that she knows I'm right, she just doesn't want to admit it yet.

"Whatever, I've gotta go. Where's your car?" I ask.

She points to the one with the zombie lying prone next to it.

"Figures." I huff, grab its arms, and drag it out of the way. "You good now?"

She shakes her head. "No." She looks around us. "What do we do now?"

I shrug. "I honestly don't know. Get to your loved ones and find somewhere safe to wait this thing out, I guess." I shrug again and turn to leave. A thought hits me and I turn back around. "Were you here with them? Your loved ones—your family I mean?"

She nods frantically, her eyes shimmering with unshed tears.

I look at the ground and then back up to her. "Do you want to come with me?" I ask almost reluctantly.

She watches me for a second or two before nodding. "Yes, I don't want to be on my own. I mean, I can be useful, I won't be a burden. I can shoot, and I can fight. I know you're just a kid, but you seem to know what you're doing."

I nod. "I'm not a kid anymore, not after what I've seen today," I say darkly. "Let's go then." I jerk a thumb to her car, not wanting to talk about it anymore. We need to get out of the open and away from here—away from civilization in general.

We both climb into her car, a silver Prius. I buckle up and watch her do the same.

"I'm Jessica," she says, turning to me.

"I'm Mathew, but my friends call me Matty."

"It doesn't feel right leaving them here," she says, to herself more than me.

I don't say anything, but wait for her to come to terms with her loss. I had a little time to mourn—though I know I'll need to mourn again soon, just not right now. Right now I need to get away from here, I need to get to safety. When five minutes passes and we still haven't moved, I turn to her.

"We have to go, Jessica."

She wipes away the tears from her cheeks. "I don't know if I can. My babies are in there." She looks toward the fairground. "My whole family." She sniffles.

I think about Daryl and Brown Eyes lying dead inside the House of Glass. I think about the man smashing his head against the glass, and the faceless man, and all the other zombie people. I think about the mother and child on the Ferris wheel and my gut twists painfully, and then I swallow down my sadness and anger.

"They're not your babies anymore. Your babies are in here now." I reach across and touch her chest where her heart should be.

She flinches against my touch but doesn't move away, silent tears still pouring from her eyes.

"And in here." I touch her head, and she moans quietly against her loss. "They would want you to survive, to live."

I pull my hand back, placing it back in my lap, and wait again. After a minute she starts the engine and begins to back out of the space carefully. She goes to flip on her lights but I stop her before she does.

"Not yet—wait till we get further away first."

She nods and continues to drive, dodging the cars and bodies the best she can in the dark. As we get to the main highway, she looks across to me.

"Where to?" She flips her lights on, illuminating the zombie-ridden road in front of us. She gasps and quickly turns them off again as one by one the zombies look toward us.

"Away from here as quick as you can would be a start," I say as she steps on the accelerator and we speed away from the funfair.

I look out my passenger window, watching the funfair fade into the distance. Thoughts of my best friend and a girl whose name I never knew are burned into my memory forever.

"Rest in peace, Daryl and Brown Eyes," I murmur.

"Pardon?" Jessica glances nervously at me.

I shake my head sadly. "Nothing."

THE BOOK NERD
One.

Susan.

I look down at the pots soaking in the sink, my hands already red and sore from all the scrubbing I've been doing. Two more plates and one pan to go. I can't contain my sigh. I scratch at the crusted food on the side of the pan with my fingernail to see if it needs a little longer to soak—finding that it does since the cooked-on food doesn't budge. I sigh again, though I know I probably shouldn't complain: after all, I was the one who offered to host the dinner party for Ken's work colleagues. If it helped Ken, then it helped him, us—me. If it meant he was happy and he left me to my own devices—left me to my books—then I was happy.

When work was quiet, he hung around the house all day, bossing me and the cat around and leaving dirty laundry all over the floor. It's always better when he's at work. Everything just runs a little smoother.

"Susan!" Ken hollers from the dining room, his loud voice echoing down the hall to me.

I roll my eyes at the sudsy water and grip the edge of the sink. His voice is like nails down a blackboard to me—everything about the man has become unbearable. Maybe that's the problem: maybe *I'm* the problem and not him. I look down at the dirty water again, my shoulders slumping, and sigh once more.

"What is it, Ken?" I ask, already knowing what it is. It's the same routine every night, regardless of if I've been slaving over the oven for most of the day. Or if I've cleaned the entire

35

house from top to bottom, so that everything was set up for him to impress his boss. Yes, it's the same routine every single night: I cook, I clean, he rules over me and the cat with an iron fist. So I know what is coming next, though I ask anyway.

"Su-san!" he hollers again as if he didn't hear my reply, punctuating my name in that way he knows irritates me.

I dry my hands on a dishtowel, turn away from the dirty pots, and head toward the living room where my husband and his boss are—better be quick before he really loses his temper with me. I make my face more pleasant as I go into the room, turning my frown upside down and giving a smile to his colleague and then to him.

"Yes, sweetie, what can I get for you?"

He scowls at me, his jowls wobbling as he talks. "I was just telling Phil here what great chocolate chip brownies you make. Thought you could whip us up a batch."

"Sweetie, it's eleven thirty. I was just about to head to bed—once I've finished the kitchen, anyway." I can't keep the lament out of my words.

Ken offers his boss a courteous smile, hefts his large frame out of his chair, and turns to me, looking me dead center so I know he isn't messing around.

"Susan, I want you to take that sweet ass of yours to the kitchen and make us some chocolate chip brownies. I won't ask you again." His nostrils flare as he adds on the last line, and it takes everything I have to not gulp loudly.

He's right: I don't want him to ask me again. I remember the last time he had to ask me to do something twice. Still have the damn scar on my right palm from it. Who knew the bottom of a pan stayed so hot even after ten minutes? Besides, maybe I should just be grateful that the rest of his co-workers have left and there's only him and his boss Phil left to cook for.

I blink back from the painful memory, my palm feeling sore. "Sure, sweetie, I'll go make some, I'm sorry. I'll have to pop out to the store and get the ingredients though." I smile at him, glad to see his anger subsiding.

"Ken, it really isn't necessary," Phil says from the opposite chair as he puffs on a fat cigar.

Ken has purposely let Phil smoke in the house, knowing how much I hate it, but I don't say anything—I never do. I'll just have to do an intensive clean tomorrow when Ken is out at work, because he hates the smell too, and he's only allowing it to further aggravate me.

I manage contain the groan of pent-up frustration residing in the pit of my stomach, and glance down at Phil. "It's completely fine. I should have made them earlier today. Besides, they really are delicious, I'm sure you'll love them." I pat Ken on the arm, and he sits back down in his chair without another word.

"There's some things on the grocery list you should pick up while you're there too." He scowls at me, but instead of explaining that I was going to go tomorrow, I nod and smile.

"Oh, and bring us some more drinks before you leave for the store." Ken looks back at Phil and continues his conversation, dismissing me. I pick up their empty glasses and head back to the kitchen.

I take back two fresh scotches on the rocks before I leave for the store, the time hitting just past midnight as I climb into our car. I drive through the darkened streets, the roads empty of anyone else stupid enough to be out at this time on a Tuesday night, and can't help the stray tears that trail down my cheeks. I don't even know how my life got to this, how I ended up in such a loveless marriage with a man I can't stand to be around—a vile, overweight bully who loves to torment me.

He didn't used to be like this—*we* didn't used to be like this. We loved each other once, before a freak accident forced Ken out of his job. He used to drive all around the country selling high end products to big companies, but after his accident, he ended up out of work for three years. For some reason, he blamed me. Or maybe he was just envious and jealous of me because I had a job. Either way, when he finally landed a decent job that would pay the bills he forced me to quit mine, insisting that we didn't need my wage now and saying that he had to prove to everyone that he was still the man of the house after relying on me for so long.

So now he's bitter and angry, full of spite and hate for me, and I for him. I don't even care that he hits me, that he mentally abuses me; after living the past two years with him bullying me, my resolve has gone and all I care about is making it through the next day without pissing him off some more. Anything for the easy life.

I should leave him, yet for some reason I don't. I'm still here no matter what he does to try and destroy our marriage. Is it the fear of him or the fear of the unknown that drives me back to him after all the abuse?

Two.

The store is quiet when I arrive, and I grab a basket and carry it to the first aisle, picking up the groceries on the list. There's nothing terribly urgent but I get it all anyway. At least I'll have more time tomorrow to get the smell of cigar smoke out of the sofa.

The radio is playing softly in the background, and I hum along to it, lost in my own thoughts as I collect my groceries. I walk to the checkout, and the young girl behind the till blows a bubble, letting it pop loudly before offering me a small smile. She's young, can't be more than twenty, with a blunt black bob and deep blue eyes.

"Busy night?" I ask politely.

She doesn't answer, but shrugs and continues to ring up the food. I bag it all up into brown paper bags, pay the young girl, and head for the exit. As I'm going out, a man is coming in. His hood is up, covering his face from view, and if it weren't for the God-awful smell I probably wouldn't have even noticed him. I prefer to keep my head down and keep to myself, especially at the time of night it is.

However, as I pass him, he reaches out a hand and I yelp, turn, and quickstep to my car across the parking lot, trying not to drop my bags as I fumble in my pocket for the keys without having to stop.

His hood is still up and it almost sounds like he's growling as he stumbles after me, so I quicken my pace, imagining the absolute worst possible scenario of being attacked and robbed by a junkie. I glance behind me seeing, that he's still following—though his pace is slow, and since I'm now flat-out running, he's lagging behind. I drop the bags at the side of my car and hit the unlock button, open the door, and quickly throw the groceries inside before climbing in and slamming the lock down on the door.

The hooded man reaches the side of the door, but it's too dark to see his face. Strangely he doesn't go for the handle but bangs his hand on the window and makes me scream. I start the engine and peel away from him as quick as I can, feeling almost certain that I just ran over his foot. Yet when I look in my rear view mirror, I can see that he has turned and is headed back to the store without even a limp.

"Shit." I slam on the brakes, making them squeal loudly on the blacktop. He doesn't notice, though, and continues. I pull out my phone with shaking fingers and dial 911, but the stupid phone won't connect and just keeps on giving me a busy signal. I slam my hand on the wheel and curse again before turning in my seat to look at the hooded man headed back into the store. The cashier is in there—there should be a security guard somewhere, but I hadn't seen him when was inside.

My chin trembles and I take a great gulp of air, almost choking on it because it seems not to want to go down my throat to feed my burning lungs. Tears well in my eyes, and before I can change my mind I slam the car into gear and reverse all the way back to the front doors of the store. It's light inside, almost glaringly bright compared to the suffocating blackness outside. I scan the store, looking out of the right-hand passenger window, not spotting the bubble gum chewing assistant or the creepy hooded junkie. I try my cell phone once more but it beeps at me, and I throw it on to the passenger seat in anger.

Unclipping my seat belt, I take a deep breath, knowing I can't leave that poor woman in there alone without any warning. We women have to stick together—and what sort of human being would I be if I didn't at least warn her? I scan the floor, looking at my discarded groceries and wondering if any of it could be used as a weapon. I rummage around, hastily pushing the things back into the bag, and check out the floor, finding Ken's tire iron under the passenger seat. I grip it firmly and slap it against my palm, cringing at the mild pain it causes.

I suck in another shaky breath and release it slowly while I watch the illuminated storefront and get ready to get out of my car. I consider the idea of just shouting from the car door to warn her, but decide that could send the guy into a panic and make the situation worse for the woman. Ken calls me a goody two-shoes, and I guess he's right. I know he wouldn't even be considering walking into a situation like this, risking his own life for someone else. But I can't just walk away from this—from her—knowing that she could be in danger. Call me an idiot or call me kind; I just don't want someone's death on my conscience.

I finally turn to my left, ready to exit the car, and am met with the face of another man—if you can call him that. His face is beaten to a pulp, swollen and bleeding. I panic, thinking that he's possibly been attacked by the same junkie that chased me, and my hand instinctively goes to the handle. But then this man hits my window with the palm of his hand and bares his teeth at me, and I let out a small yelp of surprise and jump in my seat.

His other hand comes up to hit the window and I yelp again as he begins to pound both hands on the window and growls at me. Growls! A small splinter cracks through the window and I scream as it abruptly implodes on me, showering me with tiny pieces of glass. The man reaches in and grabs at me, his hands finding purchase on my hair, and he leans in and begins to yank on my long, red locks.

I scream and pull away, the smell of him invading my nose and making me gag. I feel the metal of the tire iron in my hand and swing out blindly, feeling it hit him in several places, but his grip never loosens and he never responds in pain—not unless his constant growling could be considered that. I swing back hard as his body leans further into the car, almost leaning down onto my lap, and somehow I manage to hit him hard on the crown of his head. The sound of metal on skull makes a sickening cracking sound, and then I feel the tire iron sink into his skull.

The man stops moving with my hair still clutched in his fist, and I realize I'm screaming as I pull and tug my head to get away from him. My hand has let go of the tire iron, leaving it where it landed, embedded in his skull, and I don't know what scares me more: the fact that I am now weaponless or the fact that my weapon is still implanted in someone's head. I hear the sound of my hair ripping free from his hand, and I can finally look up at the destruction.

He's still leaning half in the car, hanging over the broken glass of the door, which is cutting into his body. Blood trails down the doorway, toxic-smelling gases escaping from his stomach cavity. His hand is closed tight around a clump of my hair, strands of it sticking up through the top of his fist. His head hangs low, the tire iron firmly implanted in his skull. Broken pieces of head and brain matter are splattered across his hair and up the length of the weapon, and the sight makes me gag. I cover my mouth as vomit rises from my throat, spraying out between my fingers and covering my lap and steering wheel in the partially digested meal I ate earlier.

I sob loudly, squeezing my eyes closed, and try to take a deep breath, but the panic won't stop rising, the smell of the dead man invading every orifice and making my eyes stream. I turn to look at him again, gagging but not being able to vomit anything out of my empty stomach. I push at his shoulder gently, trying to get him out of my door, but he doesn't budge.

I push again, putting a hand on either shoulder and feeling his body move ever so slowly. I push once again, harder this time, feeling spurred on when his body begins to slide backwards until the force of his own weight pulls him out of my doorway and I sob again at the sound of his body hitting the ground.

I take a shaky breath, staring straight ahead. Now that I'm not screaming I can hear sirens in the distance, the wails of police cars, fire trucks, and ambulances all melding into one excessively loud siren. A blast rocks the horizon, a cloud of smoke with a ball of fire underneath it exploding into the night sky. It illuminates the car park and brings the dark world back into focus.

I gasp, a low moan of terror building in the back of my throat as I stare straight ahead at the people stumbling toward me. Men, women, children—they are all coming forth as if called up from hell. Blood tracks their paths, gore and viscera hanging from different orifices.

My vomit-covered hand comes to my mouth as I hold back another scream, and just before the first blood-covered hand pounds on the hood of my old Ford Festiva, I slam the car in gear and scream away in a trail of rubber and smoke.

Three.

"Ken!" I pull the keys from the ignition and jump out of the car. It starts to roll backwards down the drive with the door still open, and I jog to catch up to it with a curse. I climb back in and pull the handbrake on before diving back out and running to the front door.

I turn the handle and push forward, but the door doesn't open and I slam into the dark wood with a pained cry. I step back in confusion and try the handle again, jiggling it in place, but it still doesn't move. I look to the window to the left of the door, seeing the curtain twitch, and I frown in confusion.

"Ken? Open the door," I say more quietly. I glance behind me to see if I've been followed, but I'm all alone, apart from the bloody evidence of my recent murder dripping down the side of my car. I squeeze my eyes closed and open them again. "Ken, open the door," I shout.

"Keep your damn mouth shut, woman," he calls back from inside.

"Then open the door," I whisper back. I look back behind me, the snapping of a twig somewhere making me feel nervous and edgy.

"I can't. How do I know that you're not infected?"

I look at him through the window, only being able to discern a small part of his face. "What are you talking about? I need help, I need the police."

"See, always bringing trouble to the door," He huffs, and even through the door I can hear his annoyance.

"It's not my fault. There was a man, he attacked me, another woman might be in trouble." I gasp as I think about the

44

poor woman that I just left. "Oh, Ken, quickly—I need to call for help for her."

"How do I know you're not one of them? One of those things that's on the news."

I glance back behind me, hearing another explosion going off in the distance. My heart feels like it's about to explode from my chest, and I don't remember the last time I felt this livid with Ken. He's finally showing exactly how much I mean to him and how selfish he really is, and where it should hurt it doesn't; it just makes me angry. I hear talking coming from inside the house and realize that Phil must still be inside.

"Phil? Open the door for me immediately," I whisper-shout.

"Don't you speak to Phil like that, woman. That's my boss and you have no right to—"

I cut him off when I kick the bottom of the door. "Open the door NOW, Ken, before I kick the damn thing down. I'm not messing around anymore." I kick the door again for good measure. I have no idea what is going on in this town tonight, but I do know that I'm about to completely lose my temper and smash a window if he doesn't open the door for me. Three years of suppressed anger are slowly bubbling to the surface, and right now all I want to do is throttle him with my bare hands. When the door doesn't open and I'm met with silence from within, I kick the door again and yell at him. "Ken, so help me…"

"Hold your damn horses, you crazy bitch. I'm opening up," he yells back.

I turn around at the sound of footsteps, but I can't see anything. The streetlights flicker and shut off. Seconds later they come back on, and I suppress the urge to yelp or scream. I hear the key in the door and the loud creak as Ken opens it up. He looks me up and down with a grimace.

"Damn, woman, what did you do to yourself?" He points at me, jumping back as I charge past him and slam the door closed.

"I was attacked, Ken, not that you care. I was attacked—twice." I shudder. "My cell phone isn't working, I need to call the police, there's a woman at the store who might be in trouble." I think about the man I buried my tire iron in. "And a man, that," I look away, "a man that I think I killed."

"Ho-ly shit, woman! You've really done it now, haven't you?" He whistles through his teeth. He follows me through to the kitchen, with Phil at his heels, as he continues to talk. "You need to get the hell out of here, I'm not getting sent to prison for hiding a fugitive."

I grab the phone off the counter and listen for a dial tone but the line is dead. Not engaged, but dead—completely silent. I slam the phone back onto its base, grab the bottle of scotch off the counter, and take a swig straight from it, relishing the burn as it slides down my throat. Slamming the bottle down, I start opening cupboards and drawers in search of weapons.

Ken comes to stand in front of me, his hands on his hips. "Did you hear me? I need you to leave or I'll be the one calling the police."

I look up to meet his gaze, noticing the sneer on his face. I cast a glance to Phil, who is still puffing away on a cigar and looking uncomfortable. My hand touches on the metal meat tenderizer in the drawer and I grip it and stand up, meeting his hateful gaze with one of my own.

"I suggest you stay out of my way, Ken, or I will be forced to do something that you will regret. Not me, I won't regret a damn thing." The mallet feels heavy in my hand, and I see Ken's gaze travel to it.

He backs up a step with a shake of his head. "You really are one crazy bitch, you know that?" He looks over his shoulder at Phil, who is staring at us in horror. "You hear all this, Phil? Because I will be pressing charges against her." He looks back to me, meeting my stare with ice-cold hatred. "Go on then, do your worst." He laughs.

I think back to all the abuse: the fists, the kicks, the bite marks, and the burning hot pan on my hand. The excuses I've made for him, the lies I've told for him, and the tears I've shed for this pitiful man. I realize how much I hate him in this moment, how much I want him dead. Not in a flippant *you're dead to me* kind of way, but a real, *I want you to be dead and gone from this earth, my life, and out of my way.*

The metal has warmed in my palm, and my hand feels twitchy to swing it and hit him across his head like I did the man in the parking lot.

Ken sneers at me again, his lip turning up in disgust. "You are pathetic, you know that?" he growls out.

I see red and swing the mallet as hard as I can.

Four.

His mocking laugh reverberates inside my head, and I scream as I lash out with the mallet. He grabs my wrist before I make impact, and snatches the makeshift weapon from my hand. He shoves me hard in the chest, and sending me flailing until I sprawl backwards, and hit my head against the corner of the open drawer. I scream again as pain shoots through my skull, and I slump to the floor, clutching a hand to my head.

"Hit me, will you, woman?" He kicks me hard in the ribs and I gasp. His foot lands heavily over and over again until I feel something snap—possibly a rib—and I scream out with a sob for him to stop.

I look up through tear-stained eyes and hold a pleading hand up to him. My vision is blurry and I can't seem to catch my breath. The air rattling in and out of my chest sounds like lumps of milkshake being sucked through a straw.

"Stop," I plead, and cough, spitting out blood and grabbing at my ribs. "Please stop, Ken."

He takes a step closer and I brace myself for another kick, but he doesn't kick me. He stares down at me, his lip curled up in disgust before he spits on me. It hits me in the cheek, his warm saliva trailing down my face.

"You are pathetic," he says, repeating his earlier sentiment and turns away from me.

I sob as I wipe off the spit, every movement sending burning pain humming through my body. I manage to drag myself to the far wall and prop myself up against it. With one hand I pull open the freezer compartment and grab a bag of frozen peas, pressing them against my ribs and hissing in pain. I push the door shut and touch the back of my head, examining my fingers and seeing blood on them. The wound feels tender but thankfully not massively serious—from what I can tell from my feeble examination, anyway.

I can hear Ken and Phil talking somewhere else in the house—possibly the living room, from the distance of their voices. The kitchen lights are bright and are burning my eyes, and all I want to do is get to bed and curl up to sleep; but after everything that has happened tonight I know that's not an option. Something bigger than what just transpired between Ken and me is happening—something in this town, possibly the country—and I need to find out what.

I grit my teeth and pull myself up to standing, taking small steps toward the bathroom. I shut the door once inside and open the mirrored cabinet, avoiding looking at my reflection. I grab plenty of painkillers and bandages, swallowing down some Tylenol using water from the faucet to lubricate my mouth, and then I strip out of my blood-and-vomit-covered cotton dress, letting it pool at my feet. I push it over to the hamper with my foot, not wanting to bend down and have to pick it up.

I look at the purple bruising already forming around my stomach and waist, and try to contain the tears that are threatening to flow down my face again. Taking a shaky breath, I begin to wrap the bandage around my middle as tightly as I can stand it to be. It hurts like hell as I do it, but the pressure and the protection of the bandage actually make it feel better once I fix it all in place with a couple of safety pins. I grip the sink as I breathe through the pain, waiting for the nausea and dizziness to pass.

I grab my bathrobe from the back of the door and put it on, biting down on my lower lip to hold in a yelp at the movement, and then I crack the door open and pad down the hallway to our bedroom. Clicking the door in place, I grab a chair and shove it under the doorknob to stop Ken or anything else from getting in here. I can hear him and Phil going at it, trying to decide plans on what's best to do, and I know that I need to hurry and get my things together before he decides to throw me to the wolves.

I don't know what is going on out there in the city, but I know that a possible broken rib, a murderous husband out for blood, and no police for backup, I am just about screwed. I open my closet and pull out jeans and a sweater. I sit on the edge of the bed as I step into the jeans, sliding them up my thighs and buttoning them up. I stare at the sweater, knowing that it's going to hurt to get it over my head. And it does. I barely contain a scream as I stretch up and pull it down over my shoulders.

A loud thump at the front of the house makes me jump and I freeze in what I'm doing, one hand still reaching for my ankle boots and the other clutching my waist. The thump sounds again and I listen carefully as Phil and Ken begin shouting at one another more heatedly. I grab my shoes and slip my feet into them as quickly as I can, grabbing a black jacket from the closet and wincing as I pull it on.

I can hear Ken and Phil charging down the hallway toward the bedroom, yelling at me to open the door. My chin trembles in fear when I realize that I left the car keys on the kitchen counter and I'm effectively trapped in this bedroom with a crazed Ken on one side of the door and newfound horrors outside of the window.

The doorknob jostles in place, but the chair stops Ken from getting in to me. "Open the door, Susan," he yells from the other side.

I don't answer him, but go back into my closet, glancing up to my hatbox on the top shelf, where I know my .38 Smith & Wesson is. The door handle jostles again and I grab the small stepladder, open it, and climb up the three steps until I can reach the box. I climb back down and place the circular box on the floor before quickly opening the lid. I got the gun several months ago—after the burning pan incident; because it was after that event that I realized the day would one day come when he wouldn't be able to stop himself. When he wouldn't be able to contain his rage against me and the world and I would be forced to defend my life. I never truly believed I would have to though, not really.

As the door handle jostles again and Ken's voice shouts to me, I know that today is that day.

I gulp and open the box of cartridges, the cold metal objects feeling foreign in my fingers as I slip five of them into the gun and close it. I pick up the box of cartridges and put them in my jacket pocket, and stand back up.

"Susan! Open the Goddamn door or I will kill your scrawny ass."

"Go away, Ken," I yell back to him. "I don't want you in here. I don't want you near me."

His foot hits the bottom of the door repeatedly but I somehow manage to contain my scream as I stand with the gun raised, ready and waiting.

"I'm not kidding, woman, open the door," he yells again.

I hear the sound of glass breaking at the front of the house and listen in horror as his kicks get more frantic.

"Open the door."

His voice sounds whiny and frightened instead of furious and scary like it did moments ago, and I bite my lip, giving in to him. I lower the gun and take a step forward, doubting what I'm doing but knowing that I can't leave him out there like that. I take another step forward and reach for the chair wedged up against the door as he shouts at me again.

"I will kill you!" he roars in anger, and starts to kick the door over and over again.

The wood begins to split and I lift the gun and take aim, stepping backwards as splinters of wood fly inwards.

"Susan! Please, open the door, please," he sobs loudly, his sob ending on a scream of panic.

I crouch down, looking through the small crack in the bottom of the door, and see several sets of feet heading toward him. Their movements are slow and shambly, blood trailing on my clean carpet. Their moans are drowned out by Ken's frantic cries and screams as they reach him and I hear him fighting— fighting for his life. All too soon I hear the sound of choking, and blood pours to the floor moments before Ken's body finally hits the blood-stained carpet. Whoever or whatever is out there drops to their knees as they crowd around him and begin to feast on his flesh.

I clasp a hand over my mouth and step away as his blood soaks under the door, saturating the carpet. I don't feel any shock that my first thought isn't one of sadness for my husband's brutal demise, but for the fact that I know my carpet is ruined.

Ken purposely picked such a light-colored carpet knowing that it would be a total nightmare to keep clean, and for three years I have done it—scrubbing and vacuuming to keep it pristine for him. It's actually satisfying knowing that he ruined it and not me, and I grin at the thought that he will be turning in his grave at that realization.

Five.

I run quietly to the window and look outside. The sound of tearing flesh and growls of hunger coming from the other side of the bedroom door are my soundtrack. I try to be as quiet as possible so as not to draw attention to myself and keep whatever is attacking—eating—Ken unaware of me in here. I shudder at the thought of what could be happening to him right now. The sound alone is enough to drive someone crazy.

Outside it's dark, the streetlights flickering on and off before finally succumbing to whatever is draining their power. The house lights go off at the same time and I stifle a scream as I'm engulfed in the blackness. Whatever is on the other side of the door doesn't seem to mind, and the feasting noises continue regardless.

Trapped in the blackness, every sound—both inside and outside the house—seems louder: the sirens in the distance, the faint screams, the *pop pop pop* sound of gunfire, and of course the tearing sound of flesh. I shudder again.

The streets seem deserted—at least this one does—though shadows move within the houses, flashlights beams skimming across windows and drawing attention to themselves. Either way, I'm still trapped in this bedroom and my car keys are in the kitchen, but at least I have a weapon.

The sounds in the hallway stop, and I pause in my inner ramblings. A low growl is issued, echoing in to me and chilling me to the core. I raise my gun, aiming it at the door at the sound of movement outside. Something slides along the door, the puddle of blood splashing and squelching underneath whatever it is. I creep forward slowly, around the edge of the bed, and crouch down to look through the small split in the

53

bottom of the door. It's so dark that I can't see anything, though' but something is definitely moving out there, and the hungry slurping noises have stopped.

Steps recede down the hall away from me, and I let out the breath I didn't know I was holding. I tiptoe across the room, my shoes squishing in the blood, and press my ear to the door. The thumping of my heart makes it hard to hear anything and I resort back to holding my breath again. I let several minutes pass by, and when I don't hear anything but deathly silence as I move the chair as carefully as I can.

Holding the .38 in my hand, I turn the doorknob slowly, praying that the door doesn't squeak on its hinges. Silence greets me and I mentally breathe a sigh of relief before I let the door open an inch further and look out. I can't see anything in the small gap, so I open the door up some more. With the only window at the other end of the hallway, and all the lights out in the house, I'm greeted by near blackness and I gulp comically loud. I can hear shuffling off somewhere else in the house, but nothing is in the hallway any longer, and I'm grateful for that.

I glance downward, not really wanting to see Ken's destroyed body but morbid curiosity getting the better of me. And okay, I want to gloat a little that he finally got what he deserved. What can I say? He was a bastard to me for the past three years, and I'm not sorry that he's dead. Of course I feel bad about the way he met his bitter end—I wouldn't wish that on anyone—but regardless, I'm happy he's out of my life now. I suck in a sharp breath when I see lumps of things scattered around the carpet, sopping puddles of blood expanding as it soaks in further; but the most frightening thing of all is that Ken's body is not there.

I look up to the end of the hallway, seeing dark shadows of bloody footprints along the floor and smears of darkness across the walls. I swallow loudly and bite down hard on my bottom lip again, tasting the metallic tang of copper on my tongue. *What the hell is going on tonight?* I can practically feel my mind trying to unravel itself, but I refuse to let it happen, to lose myself to insanity. I've survived a loveless marriage, emotional and physical abuse; I am not about to lose myself to the Goddamn apocalypse!

I gasp at the realization of that single thought.

This is it: an apocalypse. The end of days. And those things that I've tried to not give a name to, I know what they are. They are the things that haunt the worst nightmares, that movies and books are based on. Things that every horror enthusiast embraces with open arms like they're the damn Easter bunny. But these things are not friendly, this is not funny, and I refuse to be eaten by a zombie.

With that thought in mind I piece myself back together, knowing that at some point in the future I'll have to mentally decompress and work through all this; but right now I need to get to the kitchen, get my car keys, and get the hell out of here.

I clutch the .38, tightening my grip on it, and slowly tiptoe down the hallway. The smell of the roast dinner I cooked tonight is long since gone, and in its place is the smell of something sickening. It smells like meat left out in the sun for too long, a putrid and gag-inducing smell that makes my mouth turn down in distaste and bile rise in my throat. It's so fresh and pungent that my eyes begin to water, tears streaming down my face as I struggle to control myself.

I stop at the top of the stairs and look down into the darkness, I can still hear something moving about down there, but can't pinpoint exactly where in the house it is coming from. By halfway down my confidence has grown, and though I'm still frightened, I can't help but think maybe I'm making things worse with my vivid imagination. Ken always said that always having my head in a book would get me in trouble, and maybe he was right. My favorite books have always been horror: things that would normally make women cry and cower tended to make me smirk. Ken always said I was sick, that it was evil the joy I got out of horror novels, but he didn't understand me, or them, or what I got out of them.

I step down on the last step with that in mind, with Ken's bellowing voice in my head telling me what a freak I am. His large double chins wobbling as he told me how useless I was, how fat and pathetic I was, how I needed him, how he could do better than me.

I sob as his greasy hand hits me in my stomach, making me double over in pain, and I look up to meet his gaze. His eyes are almost bugging out of his head, his teeth bared, and he snarls and reaches for me again. Without a second thought, I raise the gun and fire directly into his face. My aim is accurate and makes contact exactly where I want it to, and his ugly fat head explodes as several bullets enter his skull. I'm instantly splattered with his foul-smelling blood and brain matter. His body slumps to the ground in a heap with a large thud, and I stare in open-mouthed shock before letting out a short, sharp scream. I clutch a hand over my mouth in horror as blood pools around his body, destroying yet more of his precious carpet.

A laugh builds inside of me, and I feel terrible for it but I can't control it. I try to swallow the laugh down, to stop it from escaping, but this entire night has been crazy and nothing makes sense anymore—nothing except that my stupid, big, fat, cruel husband is dead. It's not insanity that's gripping me as I step over his body, flinching only when I nearly slip in his blood. It's happiness. For the first time in three years, I feel happy.

A small smile creeps up my face, building until I'm happier than a pig in shit. I'm free of that bastard. I chuckle again as I walk into the kitchen, seeing my keys on the counter.

Everything will be fine now. I smile again. I grab a bag from the kitchen cupboard and start packing some necessities. If Ken would have allowed me, I would have been a prepper—because I knew one day this would come, and we would need to be prepared.

I work through my mental checklist of things that will be important for life on the road, packing the first aid kit, a lighter, and some of the larger kitchen knives into the bag after I wrap them in some dishtowels so they won't cut through the bag. Food is important, and I go to the garage, my hand instinctively reaching for the light switch and flipping it, and I grimace when the light doesn't come on. I open some of the drawers on Ken's tool bench, finding his flashlight and a great utility tool that might come in handy.

I move around Ken's Ford pickup truck, being careful as I usually am around his baby for fear that he'll flip his lid and yell at me for getting a smudge on the pristine paintwork. On the left side of the garage is where we keep the bottled water. Ken has always refused to drink tap water, insisting that there is mercury and lead in it and the water manufacturers are in cahoots with the government to make the population dumber. I never had the nerve to tell him that if he really believed that was the case, then there was probably no hope for him anyway.

Sitting in the corner are three cases of his favorite brand of water, and I'm thankful that I had gone to the store on Sunday and stocked up. I grab the top case, feeling the weight of the water but I'm not too concerned as I'm used to carrying it, since Ken never bothered to help. I pass back around the front of the truck and stop, looking at the shiny blue paintwork with a smile. My piece-of-shit car parked outside won't get me very far, and I can't just go and steal Phil's expensive car, but since Ken won't be using his truck anymore I don't see why it should just sit here rusting away.

I smile as I drop the water into the back of the truck. I always wanted to drive this car, but never thought I'd have the chance. Thirty-six car payments and I've never even sat behind the wheel. My grin grows bigger, my heart pounding in my chest as I load up the rest of the water and head back to the kitchen for my bag of items.

I grab the keys from the drawer by the garage door and then stop in my tracks when I turn into the kitchen and see Phil—Ken's boss—standing looking out of the window as if in deep thought. He must have been off hiding somewhere and finally come out to check on Ken. He turns to me slowly and I cry out, unable to stop the scream that erupts from my throat as I see him.

Phil growls at me and lurches forward, his arms reaching for food that he cannot possibly see with so much of his face missing, and despite the fear and horror that I feel, my first thought is that I'm never going to get to drive the damn truck.

Six.

I reach for the gun, and curse when I remember putting it down on the driver's seat inside the Ford. I grab my backpack, then turn and run, heading back to the garage to retrieve it. I slip on the bottom step and stumble down the three concrete steps, hitting my jaw hard against the concrete floor. I cry out again as my teeth smash together hard enough for me to see stars, and though I know my arms are trying to push myself upwards and back onto my feet, the rest of my body is not responding. I feel dizzy, and gag as the smell of Phil fills my nose and his pained groan of hunger calls down to me. My ribs throb painfully, the weight of Phil pressing into the bruises I know are there.

I soldier-crawl myself forward across the floor, listening to the sickening thud of Phil as he falls down the stairs. My vision swims as panic grips me, and I try to push up again only to be pushed down as Phil's body grabs me and pushes me against the concrete floor. I scream and kick out, feeling his mouth working against the back of my sweater, and I push up and flip myself over so that I'm looking up to the ceiling. He's relentless in his pursuit, like some crazed attacker as he pulls himself up my body, ignoring the kicks that I land on him.

His jaw snaps at my face, his strength greater than mine even in death. I want to cry out again at the realization that this is it—this is where I meet my end. I'm only grateful that it isn't Ken who got to finish me off. Sweat trickles from my brow as I push both hands against his chest to keep his snapping teeth away from me, trying not to look at his non-existent face. The only things remaining are his jaws and teeth; the rest looks like it has been chewed up by a pack of dogs.

As the thought hits me, I hear them: more zombies. They crowd the doorway as one by one they fall down the concrete stairs and head toward me, and this time I do scream. I scream, hit, kick, and punch until I can feel blood raining down on me and a *snap* as the palm of my hand hits where the bridge of Phil's nose should be and his head snaps back wickedly, breaking his neck bone. His mouth still snaps away as he growls, but his head is now looking up toward the ceiling instead of at me, and the small distraction is all I need to heave his body off me and drag myself to my feet seconds before the other zombies reach me.

I shuffle across the floor and under the Ford, retrieving the backpack on the way. I pull myself along until I reach the other side of the truck, and then stand up quickly and climb in, panting heavily. The keys are there on the seat along with my .38, the flashlight, and the utility tool I had found earlier, and I sob loudly in happiness, fear, and exhaustion as I push the key into the ignition and start the truck.

I stare at the metal garage door for a second before fastening my seatbelt, slipping the truck into gear, and flooring it. The truck hits the door with a screech of metal, but the door doesn't move. I slip the truck into reverse and pull away from the door as hands begin to pound the side of the truck, and then I accelerate forward again. This time seeing the door coming loose from its hinges and landing heavily on the hood of the truck.

All the zombies are now pounding the glass, growling and snapping their jaws as they try to get in at me, and I try the best I can to avoid their gaze as I accelerate forward, letting the metal door slide from the hood and to the floor. I drive over it and out into the night, leaving my prison home and asshole husband behind me.

In my mirror, I see shadows lurching out of my garage and attempting to follow me. But they soon lose interest, heading toward the front door of someone else's home. Guilt eats away at me at the thought of who is inside that house, but there's nothing I can do now. I can't save them—even if they are still alive. I wish I would have gotten to know our neighbors, but I was always too afraid that they would see my bruises and comment on them. So I kept myself to myself, and held up the pretense that everything was okay. Now as I drive away, it seems even more awful that I'll never get to know them.

*

The first couple of streets are quiet, and it's almost as if the last few hours were completely in my head, but then I snap myself back to reality. The last time I started thinking that way, a hungry and very vicious-looking Ken greeted me at the foot of the stairs and tried to eat me. I clutch a hand over my mouth as I gag on the vomit that tries to escape.

I see his face exploding in slow motion, the smash of his skull as the bullet tore through the center of his face, bone and cartilage being thrown in every direction as the bullet escaped out of the back of his head and blood splattered all over me. The truck swerves and I bump into the sidewalk, taking out a couple of garbage cans that have been put out for collection and throwing up the trash across the road. I slam on the brakes and stop, looking up to the ceiling of the truck as I try to catch my breath. The air burns as I swallow it down, trying to control my panic.

"Help, help me!"

I look to my rear-view mirror and then quickly turn in my seat. A woman is running down the street, a child clutched around her middle while a horde of hungry undead follow in her wake. She looks behind herself and then back to me, waving at me and screaming at me not to go.

I climb out of the truck, leaving the engine running, my gun in hand, and walk around to meet her. A zombie stumbles from one of the houses, shambling toward her, and I take aim and fire. Even in the dark with only the moon to offer me light, I know that I hit it. The woman runs to the passenger side and climbs in without saying anything, and I climb into the driver's side and pull away from the sidewalk, dragging one of the metal trash cans with me for a few hundred yards before it finally relents and rolls away noisily.

I drive in silence, occasionally glancing at the woman and her sobbing child. Both of them are covered in blood, and I can see the woman is shaking, her body trembling from head to toe, but I can't see any visible injuries. As I drive into the main part of town, I pass the grocery store I had been to earlier, seeing smoke rising from inside, and enough of the undead in the parking lot to fill a shopping mall, and I shudder.

"Thank you."

I look across at the woman and offer a small smile. "Is the little one okay?" I nod toward the child, who has sobbed herself into a fitful sleep.

The woman clutches the child tighter to her and nods, kissing the top of the little girl's head gently. "She's fine. Just frightened. She doesn't understand what's happening."

I watch the road, swerving around cars on fire and bodies in the way. I try not to think about the things I drive over, the sickening *crunch* always a telltale noise.

"Do you know what's happening?" she asks.

I shake my head no, my gaze drawn to the old theatre house. I stare in disbelief at the car implanted in the brickwork roughly halfway up the building. "Jesus," I mumble.

"You think this was Jesus's doing?"

I glance at her and frown. "I don't know what this is— maybe Jesus, maybe not. All I know is that things aren't going to be the same ever again. Not after tonight."

The little girl cries in her sleep, and the woman kisses the top of her head again.

"I'm Susan." I offer her my hand but she ignores it.

"Her daddy, he…he didn't want to hurt her. He made us leave. He said he knew he wouldn't be able to stop himself." Tears escape from her eyes but she doesn't wipe them away and she doesn't answer me. Instead, she turns toward the window and lapses back into silence.

As I drive through town, I see other vehicles—some filled with passengers, others with only one or two people inside. We acknowledge each other with nods of the head and sorrow-filled eyes, all of us having seen so much tonight—too much. The police station I was heading to for safety brings me back to reality with a jolt when I see it on fire, with bodies of the dead hanging around the front entrance. Some have gotten too close and flames lick up their backs; others sway silently, limbs missing and gore running free.

I look across at the child and see how much she's paled. Poor thing must have been through so much tonight. She seems settled now thankfully. Her body still almost lifeless as she sleeps soundlessly.

I keep on driving, not even bothering to slow down and ignoring their feeble attempts to follow me through the darkened streets. The town limit comes into view and I pass the sign that normally offers a cheery goodbye to any visitors. I keep on driving, not knowing where to go, where is safe, or what life will be throwing my way next. After three years of constant abuse, trapped in my prison of a home and knowing exactly what each day would bring, the thought of not knowing what will happen tomorrow or the next day is enthralling.

Freedom like I have not felt in too long washes over me and I get tingles. Yes, the horror of the day is still there; I'm aware that people have lost so much—the mother and child next to me are evidence of that, and for that I can't help but feel guilt. But for me, I can't help but look forward to each day. However numbered they may be.

I glance at the woman next to me, a small smile involuntarily playing on my lips. Her head is resting against the window, her eyes squeezed shut, sleep dragging her under. I look down at the child again and gasp. She's staring back at me, her eyes pale and lifeless, and my sadness is stolen at the sight of something so beautiful and dead in her mother's arms.

Seven.

I slam on my brakes, sending the mother and child forward in their seat as the little girl clamps down on her mother's neck, her teeth digging into the soft flesh of her mother's throat. Blood sprays out from the wound and it seems that all three of us are screaming at once, the noise overly loud in the cramped space.

The mother fights to unclamp her child's teeth from her neck, and I grab the gun from my lap and aim it at the little girl.

"Don't you dare! Don't you dare!" the woman screams and reaches for the door handle, falling from the truck with her child still attached.

I climb out and run around to the front of the truck, watching as she pushes her daughter away and stumbles backwards, one hand clutching at her throat even as blood bubbles between her fingers, tears and blood mixing across her chest.

"Layla, sweetie, it's Mama, stop, please stop," she sobs over and over.

I raise my gun again as the little girl crawls forwards on hands and knees, growling and snapping her jaws.

The mother's eyes go wide when she sees me aiming my gun. "Do not shoot my little girl!" she screams at me.

I cock the gun, my chin trembling but my hands steady. The little girl has reached her mother. She grabs at her leg, and the mother feebly tries to kick her away without harming her.

"She'll kill you," I yell back, uncertainty washing over me.

"You do not hurt my daughter," she sobs again, shuffling back once more. She looks toward the small child.

"Please Layla, I know that you're in there." She reaches a hand out to the child, her palm opening up.

The little girl looks at the hand, her pale eyes staring at the gesture of peace from her mother. She moves forward, and reaching forth she places her small hand inside that of her mother's, and I let out a sob at the same time as the woman does.

The woman looks to me. "See? See, I told you, she'll be okay—" Her words end on a scream as the little girl bites down on her fingers and I hear the crunch of teeth breaking bone—or perhaps vice versa. Either way, the mother screams in pain as blood gushes from her hand.

I take aim and shoot her daughter in the head instantly, and they both collapse in a heap.

There's a split second of silence shortly before the mother begins to painfully wail, calling her daughter's name repeatedly. She pulls the little girl's lifeless body into her lap and rocks her back and forth, kissing her head, and all I can do is stand and stare as sadness engulfs me, ripping me apart from the inside out.

"I'm so sorry," I murmur after several minutes of listening to the pained cries.

She looks up at me sharply, her skin already beginning to pale, her lips turning blue. "I told you," she chokes, coughing up blood. "I told you she would be fine." She coughs again and continues to sob.

I sit down on the ground, letting my gun fall into my lap. The blacktop is cold underneath me, but I am already chilled to the bone. Any happiness I ever thought I could have has evaporated, and I know after seeing this I'll never feel any sort of happiness again.

Rain begins to patter down on me and I take in a deep shaky breath before looking toward the mother. She's still holding her child, but at least she's stopped crying for now. She looks up, her eyes meeting mine, and I feel my own eyes fill with tears.

"It's nearly time," she whispers, and licks a tongue across her lips. There's so much blood everywhere that it's hard to distinguish where it ends in the dark.

I watch her in confusion as she continues.

"I'm dying," she clarifies. "I can feel it coming. It's starting to take over. That's how he knew." She smiles and then chokes on blood, coughing up more of it and spraying it across her daughter's lifeless form. Blood still bubbles from her neck wound but she doesn't bother to try to stop it now, as if she's given up on life. "Help me," she asks quietly.

I nod and stand, moving toward her. I put my arms around the child to lift her but the woman clings to her child's lifeless body and shakes her head, so I let go. I move to the woman, lifting her up with difficulty as she clings to her daughter. She nods to the side of the road and together we stumble over. She heads to a large oak tree and I help to slide her down it so that her back is resting against it. She pulls her daughter onto her lap again and closes her eyes as she places a kiss on her head.

"I'm ready," she whispers and takes a shuddering breath.

I stare at them, wrapped together in each other's arms, and try not to cry. The bite in the daughter's side is visible now: a large hole in her stomach that even if hospitals were taking patients, I don't think she could have survived something like that. Her mother knew all along, and yet she still held her, still loved her, still waited with her until the end. And now she wanted to be with her daughter and husband.

I raise my .38 and without a second thought and fire a hole into the mother's head.

I walk back to my truck, climb in, and put my seatbelt on before pulling away. I see a sign for an old army base and decide to try my luck there. It's some miles away yet, but I should arrive just before morning, hopefully.

I hope someone is there. I'm so tired right now.

BIG GIRLS DON'T CRY
One.

Max.

"Max, can you come into my office, please? I need you to take some notes for me on a new contract."

I look up from my bright computer screen at Mr. Slewson—my boss—with a nervous smile. I hate it when I have to go into his office. He's a total creep, always standing behind me and trying to see down my shirt. I may be blond but I'm not dumb, and I know exactly what he's doing. And he knows I know, which is worse—because really, what can I actually do about it?

I force a bigger smile. "Sure, be right there."

He slaps a hand on top of my desk over-enthusiastically. "Great, bring your pad and a pen to take notes." He winks and struts down the hallway to his office, leaving a trail of expensive and overpowering cologne in his wake.

I roll my eyes at his back, his broad shoulders stretching the rich fabric of his suit.

"I can't stand that guy." Mary, the new temp leans over from the other side of the small office booth, her chair creaking. "Total creep. Did I tell you I caught him looking at porn in his office last week?"

"You did not!" I gasp and laugh, running my pink-manicured fingers nervously through my blond waves. She's only been here for six weeks or so, but has fit right in to the office.

Our desks are arranged in small squares, segmented by conjoining desks. I share mine with Mary and Danielle. The fourth desk is stacked with trays for filing various paperwork. Since Danielle is off today with some sort of flu, it leaves just Mary and me to hold down the fort.

She nods frantically and laughs. "He was totally beating one off in there."

"Ewww, gross out!" I giggle. I look toward his now closed door, and watch his shutters flick down so no one can see in, and I grimace. "Better get going, huh?" I stand and straighten my skirt, fixing my blouse so that it doesn't come down as low.

"Max?"

I look back at Mary and force a smile. "I'll be totally okay, don't worry."

The thing is, the air conditioning hasn't been working the past six weeks. We're on the top of a twelve-story building and as such, are slowly roasting to death up here. There's a fine line between appropriate dress and slutty, and I normally manage appropriate—just about—but with the heat, it was hard not to look slutty.

I pick up my legal pad and Parker pen and take the walk of shame to his office—shame because every woman in this place knows what he's like, and what I'm in for. Each face holds a small smile of sympathy and some relief. There's only one bitchy smirk, which I try to ignore: Helena. Deep down I know she sympathizes, but she's always been jealous of me—like it's my fault that I was graced with an hourglass body and pouty lips. It's like high school all over again, with the dirty looks and always trying to get me in trouble. The only difference is that this time we're not fighting over boyfriends. She's happily married and I'm more than happy with my long-term girlfriend Constance.

I smile as I pass Helena's desk, always determined to be polite and kind no matter what. Mamma always told me that they've won if they made you lower yourself to their standards. And I refuse to lower myself to her standards.

I knock on Mr. Slewson's door gently, pressing my pad nervously against my chest as I wait for him to reply. I know that I'll be here for a minute or two. That's just another one of his tricks: he likes to show his importance by keeping people waiting at his door for him.

That, or like Mary said—he's beating off in there.

A minute goes by and I knock again.

Two minutes, and I clear my throat loudly to remind him that I'm still waiting out here.

Three minutes, and I turn to go back to my desk when I finally hear his deep voice tell me to come in.

I roll my eyes, force a smile, and push open the door. "Hi, Mr. Slewson."

His cheeks look flushed, even with the small fan behind his desk throwing semi-cool air over him. "Please, take a seat, Max." He gestures to the chair in front of his large oak desk and leans forward as his gray eyes follow me across the room.

I sit and cross my legs, resting my pad on my lap. I pull out my pen and click it on, and look up with a smile. "Ready, sir."

He watches me for a second, running a hand through his hair. The air is stale in here, stale and sweaty with an underlying scent of something I don't want to think about. I look back up when he doesn't speak, and watch as his mouth twists up into a slow smile.

"You're ready, huh?"

I nod. "Yes, sir." I smile again patiently.

"I bet your boyfriend loves you being ready, huh?"

I swallow slowly. "Excuse me, sir?" I frown, heat spreading across my neck.

The air has stilled around us, despite the fan still shuffling his papers every now and then as the oscillating head continues to turn from left to right and from right to left. My lashes feel heavy. Damn store didn't have my usual brand and so I had opted for a cheaper pair, but I'm regretting it now in this sticky office.

"I like it when you call me sir." His mouth quirks up in a sleazeball smile that makes me want to gag. I have no idea what to say to that, or where to look for that matter; it's all getting far too uncomfortable for my liking.

Mr. Slewson suddenly barks out a deep laugh, making me jump and let out a little squeal. He stands and comes around his desk, adjusting his pants as he does, and I grimace as Mary's words once again ring in my mind. He leans backwards against the oak desk, his butt perched at the edge, and he crosses his arms, all the while continuing to watch me with a smirk. I hadn't realized that my chair was so close to the desk, and now with him standing there, his crotch is eye level with me. I lean back as far as possible but try to act natural about it.

"You wanted me to take notes for you, about the last contract I typed up." I look away from his sly grin, feeling the blush spread further up my neck to my cheeks. His eyes rove toward my heavy chest, and I feel embarrassment flare even more.

"I bet you keep your boyfriend happy, don't you, Max?" His tongue slips across his lips, his nostrils flaring. I don't know if he's trying to be seductive or not, but it's not attractive. "Yeah, I bet you're a real man-eater, aren't you?" he chuckles.

"Mr. Slewson." I clear my throat again, embarrassed and unsure why I'm going to tell him the next thing, but hoping that the small truth will make him back off a little. "I, umm, I like to think I keep my girlfriend very happy." I smile shyly, waiting for the penny to drop.

I've never kept it a secret that I'm gay, and I've never been embarrassed about it, but it's also not something I feel the need to openly talk about. Why would I? But the minute the words leave my mouth, I know that it was a huge mistake mentioning my sexuality to him, and I want a hole to open up beneath my chair and swallow me up.

"You're a rug-muncher?" He claps his hands together and barks out another laugh. "So, you only float the lady boat, huh?" He grins and looks away for a moment, his thoughts no doubt going somewhere disturbing. He finally looks back to me, adjusting his pants again. "So have you ever been with a man?" He narrows his eyes and leans down to me. "I mean, have you ever thought that maybe you've never met the right man?" He grins and leans further forward, breathing heavily in my face and making me want to gag when I smell the onions he's had for lunch.

"Sir?" I squeak out.

He stands and walks behind me, his trademark move.

I grimace.

"You know, if you do ever want to try out some prime meat from the butchers' counter instead of something from the fishmongers, I'm a willing participant."

His hand touches the back of my neck and I stand abruptly, bumping his mouth against my shoulder in an angry clash of teeth as I do.

"Motherf…" he yells out.

I turn around quickly, watching as he clasps a palm across his mouth. "Ohmygod, ohmygod! Mr. Slewson, I'm so sorry." I grab some tissues from the box on his desk and hand the wad to him to dab the blood dripping from his mouth.

"I think you chipped a toof! I bet you did that on murpose," he slurs with a scowl. "Fucking dyke."

I didn't do it on purpose, but I really wish I had, and I fight to stop the smile spreading across my face. "No, sir, no, it was an accident. You just made me jump,"

You pervert.

He scowls harder, but is interrupted from speaking when a scream sounds out from the hallway. He turns to look at the doorway, turning back to me with a frown.

"Damn women, always so temperamental." He looks at the tissue in his hand. "Get me some fucking ice," he slurs, and heads back around to his chair.

"Yes, sir, yes of course."

"And see what the hell's going on out there." He pulls out a mirror from his desk, opens his mouth wide, and begins to examine the inside to check the damage.

I grab my pad from the floor and scurry out of the office, clicking his door shut behind me with a heavy sigh. I head back to my desk, throwing my pad on top, and frown as I look over at Mary's desk and see all her things tipped over. If there's one thing about Mary it's that she's a neat freak.

Glancing around me, I finally notice the disarray of the entire office, and the distinct lack of people. I walk away from my desk and toward the break room, seeing that the door is shut, and it's never shut. Damn door creaks louder than anything, so it's always wedged open.

Except now.

I frown hard at it and then stop myself: frowns give you wrinkles. My hand presses down gently on the handle and I push the door inwards slowly, the creak almost deafening in the quiet of the office. I peer around the door, gasping as twenty sets of wide eyes stare back at me from behind the upturned desk where we normally eat our lunch.

"Everything K?" I ask as I look them all over with a cautious smile.

Two.

"Have they gone?" Eleanor whispers to me, staying behind the table with everyone else.

I look behind me, back into the open-plan office. "Have who gone?" A chill runs across my arms, and I wish for the second time today that I would have worn something that showed less flesh.

Eleanor comes around the table, her brown eyes fearful. "Those…things."

I smile at her. "Sweetie, are you okay?" I reach a hand out to touch her shoulder, but pull back when I see the blood on it. "What happened to you? Should I go get someone from first aid for you?" My eyes look to everyone else in the room, finally noticing their panicked expressions. "What's going on? This isn't some sort of prank, is it? Like Ashton Kutcher isn't going to jump out on me or anything, because it's not funny. I hate scary movies. My girlfriend is always pulling this sort of thing on me, and I don't like it one bit." I let my words trail off as I frantically look around the room for hidden cameras.

A high-pitched scream pierces the air, and Eleanor rushes forward and shoulder barges me out the way. Her hands slam the door shut, the long, drawn-out creaking from the hinges seeming even more ominous now. She grabs my hand and we back away from the door.

"What's going on?" I whisper, my heartbeat becoming frantic.

"Shhhh!" Eleanor hushes me quietly and takes another step back from the door as a shadow falls underneath it.

The air stills, and I hear a collective intake of breath as we all stare raptly at the shadow. I want to open the door, to tell them all to stop doing this now because I don't like it one bit, but I don't. Instead I cling onto Eleanor's hand as if my life depended upon it, and I stay as still as I can, all the while watching the shadows along with everyone else.

Minutes pass, and the shadow of whoever was outside the door leaves. I expect everyone to laugh and to start to chatter noisily like normal, probably bitch about Eleanor for scaring the heck out of us, but no. No one says anything. No one moves. No one speaks, and there is definitely no one laughing.

I turn to face them all, taking in their fearful expressions.

"Come on, girls. This is silly. Tell me what's going on." When no one answers me, I turn to Eleanor. "Come on, what's going on? I don't think this is funny now."

Her eyes are brimming with tears, her chin trembling, but she doesn't say anything.

"This is ridiculous. I have to get some ice for Mr. Slewson," I pout.

I step toward the door, but can't make the second step. My heart continues to beat its uneven rhythm, and I squeeze my eyes shut, take a deep breath, and finally take another step forward.

"Don't open the door," whispers someone from behind me, but I don't know who it is. "Please don't open the door."

I've listened to these women talk for years, I know every one of their little speech quirks—the sounds of their voices, their accents, what they sound like angry because of pervy Mr. Slewson, or sad after a break up—and yet, I don't recognize this voice. Because this voice is laced with fear, and I've never heard any of their voices filled with fear before.

My chin trembles even though I try to contain it, and regardless of the fear-filled voice I take another small step forward. Whatever is out there, it can't be that bad, surely. My hand touches the handle, and I glance over my shoulder with a small smile.

"Look, ladies. I don't know what's got you girls all in a tiz, but if we can face Mr. Perv on a daily basis, we can handle this...problem." I choose my words carefully. "I'm sure whatever you saw is not as bad as you think it is. It's that thing that you hear about, like sheep mentality or whatever. You've just all freaked yourselves out or whatever. Now come on, chins up, let's face this together."

They murmur between themselves, the fear finally dissipating from the room, and slowly they creep forward themselves, still unsure, but looking more confused than petrified now. I nod and smile at them, finally feeling confident again as I face the door, turn the handle, and open it up.

The creak is loud and echoes around the empty office, I square my shoulders instead of flinching like I want to. My eyes cast over the threshold. Apart from the drone of the computers in the background, which we don't normally hear because of all the chatter, everything seems perfectly normal. Well, apart from the fact that we're all huddled in the lunchroom together, of course.

I turn back to face the girls. "See, it's all K, nothing to worry about." I smile and straighten out my skirt, only flinching when Eleanor begins to scream so loud I want to shake her. "Eleanor!" I gasp.

A hand grabs the back of my blouse and I hear its distinctive tearing sound as I pull out of the grasp and turn around to face a horror like I've never seen before. Worse than when my brother dressed up like Freddy Kruger and hid in my closet on my sixth birthday. And worse than when I saw a cat get run over, making its little kitty cat insides tumble out all over the blacktop. And way worse than when my girlfriend

Constance chopped her pinky finger off with a knife and lost it in the mixed green salad she was prepping for our dinner.

A man stands before me—if you can still call him that. Tall, dark, and wearing a business suit, and if that were the entire image there would be nothing to worry about. I mean, that's the image of an ideal man, apparently. But he isn't the ideal man. Both his cheeks have been torn away so much that I can see the tendons inside his face working as he snaps at me. One eye is dangling uselessly from its socket, swinging against his cheek as if trying to look down my top and stare at my breasts. *Some men never change.*

With his one good eye he manages to get a fix on me, and growling like a rabid dog, he steps forward, reaching for me with bloody and gnarled hands. I duck underneath his arms with a squeal and dive out into the hallway, almost tripping on the carpet. Without stopping, I begin to run down the hallway to the fire exit, with piercing screams erupting behind me.

I'm thinking of my own safety—my own life, because this is not how I envisioned my death to be. It was supposed to be beautifully tragic—glamorous almost—not ugly and bloody. I stop, leaning back against the wall as the screams echo along the length of the hall to me. My chin trembles as I struggle to comprehend what the hell that *thing* was. The screams grow more panicked, rising in pitch until I think my eardrums are going to burst. I put my hands over my ears to block out the sound, but it doesn't work, and tears begin to fall from my eyes and trail down my cheeks.

The fire extinguisher is in front of me, dusty and unused against the far wall, glaring at me like a beacon of hope. I grab it, yank it from its place, and turn back to go and help my friends. The man-thing has pounced upon one of my co-workers—Tonya, I think her name is, from accounting. He's holding her against the floor while he buries his face into the crook of her neck as if he's trying to seduce her, but he's not. The blood spurting out from her is throat is a dead giveaway of his lack of amour for her. I step forward and raise the extinguisher high above my head. I may not be the strongest girl in the world, but all the yoga and Pilates I do gives me great core strength and my arms are toned as hell—totally knew it would be worth it one day. I can't wait to tell Constance that it wasn't a total waste of time.

"Get off her, you jerk!" I yell and slam the extinguisher down on his back; not wanting to go for the head and get arrested for murder.

He falls forward, the sound of broken bones issuing out much louder than I would have expected. But it doesn't stop him, not even a little bit. Instead, he looks back over his shoulder at me, snarls with his bloodied mouth, snaps his broken teeth and pushes himself up from the floor. The broken bones in his back make him stand at an odd angle, but it doesn't stop him from coming forward. He doesn't even seem like he's in any pain.

I want to scream—a loud, shrill, high-pitched pathetically girly scream that would break glass and eardrums alike—but I don't. Instead I swallow down my childlike fright and try to think of what to do. The fire extinguisher drops heavily from my limp fingers and I take a step back as he takes another clumsy step forward, his hands reaching for me in a robotic yet perverted kind of way. An image of Mr. Slewson flashes in my mind, and with a firm nod of my head to ground myself in the moment and not get lost in my own panic, I turn tail and run, making sure that this evil man-thing is following.

I know where I'm going as I run, and I know I should probably feel bad about it, but I don't. Mr. Slewson can deal with this problem. After all, he's the boss.

Me? I don't get paid nearly enough.

Three.

I run in my little black kitten heels, constantly tripping in them. They were bought specifically to look cute with my office wear, not for running from monsters! I check over my shoulder again to make sure that he's still following me; he is, leaving a trail of blood behind him like we're in some crazy horror movie. Jeez, I guess we are.

I pass my desk, only now really taking in the devastation of my small booth and wondering how I missed this previously. I glance around the office as I run, noticing overturned chairs, blood smeared across desks, and all the once neatly stacked paperwork is upturned onto the floor. Over by Caroline's desk is another one of these weird cannibal men. I shiver and give a loud wolf whistle to get the second man...thing's attention. He looks up from whatever he was doing and begins to stumble toward me. I'm both relieved and horrified that he's following me, because blood trails down his chin like he's spilled a Bloody Mary cocktail down himself.

I jog down to the end of the hallway and arrive at Mr. Slewson's door. Each side of the hallway is adorned with gold-framed pictures of him winning different types of awards or shaking hands with different famous people. The entire thing feels so overindulgent, like a walk of fame, with Mr. Slewson being the prize at the end—and even in this intense situation I can still manage a roll of my eyes at the obnoxiousness of it all. I knock lightly when I reach his door (old habits die hard) and chance a quick glance behind me. I can hear but not see the weird men, since they haven't quite turned the corner yet.

I knock on the door again, harder this time. "If that's Max then come in. Anyone else can piss off until later this afternoon," his voice yells from within. "I'm busy."

I glance behind me once more and see that the two bloodied men have just turned the corner and are following me down the hall of fame. I straighten my skirt down as I enter— again with old habits. The door swings wide open, and I open my mouth to speak but pause when I see Mr. Slewson. He's lying across the top of his desk, resting up on one elbow and wearing nothing but a tie and an award-winning smile that shows off his bleached white teeth.

"Mr....ummm." I frown, feeling a hot blush creep up my cheeks despite the fact that there are two cannibal-type men behind me, and I try not to look at his erect penis. "I ummm…"

He smiles again and sits up, his legs swinging over the edge of his desk. His fan still turns from left to right, blowing his hair as if he's on some crazy naked fashion shoot. "I figured that you owed me. After all, you've chipped my tooth, and that is going to be seriously expensive to fix." He jumps down from his desk, his butt making a loud squeaking sound as it slides against the wood, and he strides toward me, his penis bobbing with each swaggering step and making me want to vomit. "And I think you'll find it beneficial to both of us. This could vastly improve your chances of promotion of course." He stops in front of me and sneers. "Best shut the door, darlin', before someone sees all the things we're about to do to one another."

He reaches across and runs a hand down my cheek, and I nearly miss the telltale growl of dead-man-walking behind me. I flinch away from Mr. Slewson's fingertips and he scowls at me, his hand gripping my shoulder and tugging me inside. He pushes the door to close it, but I manage to slip out of one of my shoes and leave it blocking the doorway and stopping it from latching as he leads me over to the desk.

"Enough of this cock-teasing, Max. It's time to show you what a man can do." He scoffs at me, and even though fear has shot up my throat and is threatening to spill out of my mouth any second, I don't. I see the thrill in his eyes and I pale at the dark expression on his face, but I hold the ace card—he just doesn't know it yet. "I know you're going to love this, so just relax and enjoy the ride. I've never had any complaints before."

He pushes me, bending me over the desk, and I bite back a whimper as my face slams onto the warm wood where his ass just sat. He's so busy with eager hands pulling at my skirt that he doesn't hear the sound of the door creak open. His hands grab at my panties and start to tug them down, and he misses the slow shuffle of undead steps coming toward us.

If I wasn't so scared I'd smile, but that doesn't stop me from being pleased at my plan and what I have no doubt is about to happen next.

Men: they always underestimate the blonde. Assholes!

I take a deep breath and force a smile. He notices it, and his hand pushes my locks away from my face. "That's the spirit. I knew you'd see sense eventually. You just needed a real man to show you the way." He leans down and licks the side of my face, and I gag at the smell of his breath and the feel of his erection pressing against my ass cheeks. "I'm going to show you a good time, Max."

"I told you Mr. Slewson, my girlfriend already shows me a good time." I look to the floor and see feet, and with a hard push up, the back of my skull connects with his nose for the second time today. I see stars as our skulls connect, my vision swimming as I push away from the desk and him and nearly trip on my underwear around my ankles.

He yells out a mouthful of curse words, but they are suddenly drowned out by the sound of his screaming. I turn to see both bloodied men attacking Mr. Slewson, dragging him to the floor and biting into his body. He looks up at me frantically, his hands, only a moment ago greedy to get into my panties, now reaching up for me to help him.

"Max!" he yells loudly. "Max, help me. Get these fucking things off me!"

I lock eyes and smile at him as I pull my panties back up. "Sorry, Mr. Slewson, but this isn't in my contract." I step around him and the cannibal men as quick as I can and head to the door on shaky feet. I reach the doorway and slip my AWOL kitten heel back on and straighten out my skirt as I look back in at him.

His face is pale, and blood bubbles up out of his mouth as one of the men bites down on his throat, cancelling out his gargled scream.

"Let me know if there will be anything else, Mr. Slewson. I'm going to take an early lunch." I click the door shut behind me and head back down the hallway, barely holding onto my sanity as I struggle to control my manic laughter.

I turn the corner at the end, and my laughter erupts into screaming as hands grip onto my shoulders and I stare into cold blue eyes.

Constance slaps my cheek hard, and I stop my screaming and dive into her arms. She holds me tight against her chest and I breathe in her familiar scent until my heart rate dips to something more normal.

I pull back and look into her face. "Are you okay? What are you doing here?" I trace a small scratch on her cheek, and she winces and pulls away. "There are some men here. They're sick, Constance, we need to get help."

"I'm fine, but I don't think help is coming anytime soon." She smiles at me, her usual cool, collected self despite the situation. "I was at work and heard what was going on, it's all over the radio and TV. There was no way I wasn't coming to get my girl." She kisses me and smooths my curls back from my face. "We need to get out of here, babes. This disease or whatever it is, it's spreading, and quickly."

I nod. "I need to get my things from my desk." Banging from Mr. Slewson's office draws Constance's attention behind me.

"Does someone need help?" She frowns, her dark brows pulling together.

I shake my head frantically. "Hell, no. There's…" I pause, trying to decide what to call them, but as usual Constance knows what I'm thinking and fills in the gap.

"Zombies."

"Really?" I cock my head to one side, not really wanting to believe it. "I don't think they're zombies. That seems ridiculous." I scoff.

"I don't want to panic you, but after what I've seen on my way here, what I saw on the news…" She trails off before continuing. "Max, I saw a group of those things rip a man in half and start chowing down on him without a second thought. The police don't seem to have any control over what's going on right now either. It's a shit storm out there."

"Constance!" I screech, hating to hear her cuss.

"Sorry, babes. But it really is a shit storm." She shrugs, but at least has the decency to look guilty. She takes my hand and leads us to my desk, where I grab everything I might need and drop it all in my large Dior handbag while Constance patiently waits for me.

"Okay, let's do this. I know a place in the country we could go. It's far out, secluded from most places. We could stay there for a while. Ooh, you might want to open the door to the break room, there's a bunch of girls trapped in there. I hit one of those…zombies with the fire extinguisher and then had it chase me to my boss's room." I unpin a couple of pictures of my parents and Chi-Chi, our Chihuahua, and put them into one of the side pockets while Constance continues to stare at me. I glance up at her. "What?"

She grins and shakes her head. "You just continue to surprise me every day, baby." She wanders off toward the staff room, and I can't help but smile and feel all fuzzy and warm at her words.

A couple of minutes pass, and I'm all but done with packing up my things, making sure I have the essentials—like my No.5 Perfect Pink nail polish and my Chanel perfume. Priorities: looking good and not dying. Check!

Constance comes back with a gaggle of women following her; she smirks as they scatter to their individual desks to gather their belongings.

I smile as she comes back over to my desk.

"What are you looking so happy about?" I sling my bag over my shoulder and move around to her side. "Zombies or whatever are roaming the country and you seem pretty happy about it."

"You." She looks at the other women and then back to me and I notice some of the stares that I'm getting.

"Me? Why?" I giggle, wanting to be let in on the joke.

"They told me what you did. That you beat that zombie thing over the head with the fire extinguisher. You're like freaking She-Ra or something. Here I was thinking that you were this dainty-looking thing that needed looking after and possibly saving and you're here beating monsters and saving lives." She laughs and pulls me into her arms. Her lips press against mine, parting them slightly as her tongue invades my mouth, before pulling back. "You're amazing, you know that, Max?"

A blush creeps back up my neck and cheeks. "Thank you, Constance. I'm glad that you're here with me, but yes, I have no doubt that I can take care of myself."

"I have no doubt either, baby." She repeats my words and kisses my lips again, and we turn as one to look at the approaching women.

"How did you get up here?" Eleanor asks. She's tall and lithe with a neat brown bun tied at the nape of her neck. I always thought she was stuck up until today. Now I think maybe she was just a little shy, and I feel bad for jumping to conclusions on her. "I need to get to my husband." Her eyes fill with tears. "Oh God, I hope he's still at home. He works shifts, he should be sleeping now. He'll have no idea what's going on if he wakes up." With each word spoken, her voice gets a little higher, as if just by voicing it she's freaking herself out.

"It's K, Eleanor. I'm sure he's still sleeping. We'll get out of here and you can go check on him. Let's not panic." I use my soothing voice, but it only seems to agitate her further.

"Easy for you to say. You have your partner here with you. We have families that we need to get to—pets, children even. Oh God, my brother has a little girl, she'll be at day care." Another co-worker puts an arm around her shoulder and she begins to sob.

I bite my lip, refusing to argue with her. I have family: my mother and father, and Chi-Chi of course. She's at home, and we'll have to go and get her before we go to my parents' house. Constance is estranged from her family, so I know she won't want to go there—which is good, because less stops means we'll be safer.

I've seen all the horror movies, and I've read the survival books. My secret addiction to apocalypse survival is going to pay off after all. I have my bug-out bag ready to go in the bottom of my closet, and go we will—just as soon as we find out how to get out of here. I look across at Constance with a smile. I can't wait to see what she thinks when she sees my bug-out bag.

Four.

We huddle together as we tiptoe down the stairs. Every time someone gasps, the entire chain of people stops in fear, all poised and waiting to see what will happen next. We continue down the concrete steps once more, the sounds of our slow shuffles echoing down the dark stairwell. Each of us are using our mobile phones for a light, casting eerie shadows across the plain gray walls.

"Ladies, if you could all just keep calm," I ask in a polite whisper. "We'll be out of here in no time, and you can all get home to your families."

Constance squeezes my hand and keeps on walking, the slow shuffle of ladies trailing behind us.

We reach the lower stairwell, and I see dark stains smeared around the doorframe and pooled at the floor. I glance at Constance, but she's focused on the doorway, taking deep breaths to steady her nerves. She turns to look at me and then the other women before speaking.

"You need to prepare yourselves—it's dangerous out there, I'm talking really dangerous." She swallows and ties her hair back and away from her face as she continues talking. "Do you all have your car keys and know where you are headed? When we leave here, it's everyone for themselves."

I hear some gasps, and a part of me wants to scold Constance for being so heartless, but deep down I know that she's right, and I haven't even seen the outside yet.

"Let's do this," I say firmly, more to her than anyone else.

These are my co-workers—my friends, for all intents and purposes—and I wouldn't wish harm upon any of them, but I have Constance to worry about, and Chi-Chi. My poor baby will be so scared, and I need to get to her and make sure she's safe.

Constance grips my hand tightly, her fingers entwining with mine. She leans over to me and presses her lips firmly to mine. "You stay with me, no matter what."

I nod but she doesn't seem satisfied.

"You do not leave my side," she says even firmer.

"Okay," I say seriously. Like I was ever going to be anywhere but at her side at the end of the world.

I hear sniffles and hiccupping sobs behind me as Constance turns the handle on the door, pushing it open wide and letting in the world of crazy that has now become the outside.

I look back once, and mouth goodbye to my friends before I'm pulled out of the doorway and I'm running in kitten heels across a sidewalk scattered in body parts and bloody gore. Screams echo out all around me but I focus only on Constance, on her footsteps, on her hand in mine pulling me forward, and I try not to be distracted by everything happening around me. But so much is going on.

People are being wrestled to the ground by mobs of people—zombies, whatever. Rivers of blood trail the gutters, with stray limbs and bones picked clean of flesh. My stomach flips and turns, but I refuse to be the weak woman in this story. I refuse to die like this.

It's far too ugly a death!

"Max!"

I hear my name screamed out as a hand claws down my back. I stumble and trip, crashing down hard on my knees and feeling my stockings run and blood flow from my cuts. Hands latch onto my curls, and I instinctively lean back the way I'm being pulled.

91

A face leers over me, teeth gnashing together, cold gray eyes staring into me as its nostrils flare. My hand reaches out for anything, my fingers finding purchase on something both equally soft and hard. I swing back with it, hitting wildly, until the thing connects with the monster that has me in its clutches. It's not until a spray of blood cascades down on my face that I realize my weapon was once someone's leg and I yelp loudly.

The thing is suddenly dragged away from me, taking a clump of my hair with it. I scream and release the bloody leg, my hand instead gripping my head where I'm sure there is going to be a bald spot. I stumble to my feet and see Constance beating the zombie-man-thing with a better weapon than I had: a bloodied baseball bat. It's stopped moving, but she's still beating it wildly.

I grab her arm, and she stops and looks up at me with a small whimper. Blood is splattered across her face, probably much like mine, but she doesn't focus on that and neither do I.

"Let's go," I say with a shaky breath.

It takes her a moment to process my words, but she eventually nods. I take the bat from her hands, keeping a firm grip on it despite the blood that trails down the handle and under my nails. I notice that Constance's arm is cut up pretty badly, though it doesn't look like a bite.

"Are you okay?" I ask fearfully. I tear the bottom of my blouse and wrap it around the wound as she gasps in pain.

"Yeah, damn thing clawed my arm like it was Wolverine or something." She inhales as I tie the material tightly.

A sharp scream makes me look up and I see Helena stumbling toward us with one of those things chasing after her. It's slow as it shambles towards her, reaching for her with arms covered in blood and sores toward her, but she's slower. She catches my eye, her chin trembling as a thin streak of blood trails down from the top of her head, down the side of her face.

In that moment I feel so much pity for her, and I put aside all of our differences. None of it matters anymore—the snarky remarks, the horrible looks, the meanness that she always exhibits for me. I couldn't care a less about it, because we're women, and women should stand by each other no matter what. I jog forward, swinging the bat hard and smacking the man chasing her on the side of his head. It falls to the ground, still writhing around, but ultimately it—he—is out of action, at least for now.

I reach a hand down to Helena and she takes it with a sob, coming to her feet and wrapping her arms around me.

"Thank you, God, thank you," she cries.

I look back to Constance, who takes my hand once again and all three of us head toward Constance's car, which is parked across the road. I say 'parked,' but it's kind of squished in between two cars, one of which is so far into the back end of Constance's Ford that I know without a doubt it just ruled out being our getaway car.

Five.

"My car..."

I look at Helena, who is trembling from head to toe. Her hand is pointing toward the small car park across the road.

We all begin moving at a brisk pace, even as Constance asks her if she has the keys. Helena reaches into her pocket and holds them up with shaking hands. Constance reaches for them, only for Helena to snatch them away at the last second.

Constance scowls at her. "Give me the damn keys," she yells, attracting more of those things to our location.

We continue to run, hopping over the small wooden fence that surrounds the parking lot. It's only knee high, more for decoration than anything else, and so won't hold off any of those things that have now started to follow us.

We stop by a small red sports car and Helena watches me over the roof of it. "I'm sorry, Max. I never much liked you, but I wouldn't wish this upon anyone." Her words come out shaky but determined. "But it is what it is, and this is my car, and hopefully you can keep them distracted so that I can get away safely. Again, I'm so sorry about this."

"Are you serious?" Constance yells. "She just saved your life and now you're going to just leave us here to die?"

Helena shrugs, a small smile crossing her face. "I'll always be grateful for that."

"If you unlock those doors, we're getting in!" Constance yells again, desperation tingeing her words. "Do you hear me? Just try and stop us."

I look around us and see bloodied people beginning to stumble toward us. I place a hand on her arm. "Just leave it—

leave her. We'll find another way home." I step away from the car with a deep sigh.

"No, Max, she can't do this to us." Constance glares across at Helena, her eyes being drawn to the many people heading in our direction. "I will kill you," she finally says and takes my hand. Together we step away from the car.

Helena smiles. "In another lifetime maybe." She unlocks the car and climbs in, and moments later the car roars to life and wheel spins away. "Ciao, bitches," she laughs out of her window.

"Shit," Constance says, her eyes darting around us.

"Constance," I grumble, feeling suddenly exhausted. "I hate it when you cuss." My hand is still gripping the baseball bat, but from the amount of these people—things—coming toward us, it won't do any good.

"We need to get a car," she says and begins to drag me away from the mob that is getting perilously close. "Stay close, baby."

We try door after door of various cars, but they're all locked. It's not until we come to the small deli around the corner where I used to buy my lunch that we see an escape from this hellhole. Unfortunately, it wasn't an escape for the owner. The small deli delivery van is still parked outside, though the owner, Georgio Belatini—or what's left of him—is in several pieces. Thankfully, none of the pieces are moving. We avoid eye contact with the dismembered head as we rummage through his body parts and root through his pockets for the keys to the van, eventually finding them in the gutter by the wheel.

Climbing inside and locking the doors, we both breathe a deep sigh of relief. We are far from safe, but starting the engine and leaving the horde of zombie people behind us definitely makes me feel a helluva lot better about our survival chances.

Heading out of the city and toward home to collect Chi-Chi, we see many car crashes, and it takes Constance's awesome driving skills to get us out safely. All those times playing Grand Theft Auto with her brothers came in handy after all.

In my mirror I see the city burning, and finally feel a little safe—if only for the present. God knows what the future holds. On our way out of the city we pass a small red sports car that's crashed into the railings at the side of the road. The driver's side window is smashed in, and blood trails down the door, but I don't see any bodies around. I can't help but smile and think how much I love karma.

She's a bitch, but only to those that deserve it.

Hey, maybe she's blond.

GHOST TOWN.
One.

Dean and Anne.

"Okay, class, if you can open your books to page two-hundred and fourteen so that we can get started on today's assignment, please. Anyone who didn't do their homework is really going to struggle with this, because part of the work was covered with it." Mr. Jeffreys says with a trace of a smug smile.

I grab my book and flip to the relevant page with a heavy sigh. I did do the homework, but that doesn't mean any of it stuck in my head—because after completing it I had gone on to have another huge argument with Mom and Dad. It's becoming a regular thing.

"Psst."

I look across at Stephanie, my best friend. She smiles and gestures for me to hand her my homework. Unlike me, she has the perfect home life: loving parents, great big brother, and a huge trust fund waiting for her at the end of high school. She is also as dim as a box of broken bulbs, but by God she's pretty. Graced with long blond locks, crystal blue eyes, and a figure to die for, she's a living, breathing Barbie doll.

"What, Steph?" I grumble, knowing perfectly well what she wants.

She rolls her eyes. "Give it up," she hisses with a pout.

I huff and begrudgingly hand her my homework: *The greatest works of Shakespeare*. I can only hope she doesn't copy it word for word like last time and get us both into trouble, but there's no point in telling her that since she never listens.

I look up as the classroom door opens and the school secretary Mrs. Marsh comes in looking pale and shaky, a light sheen of sweat across her forehead. She scurries over to Mr. Jeffreys, casting the class a concerned look. I watch them whispering frantically for a few minutes before Steph throws my book back on my desk and makes me jump.

I grab the book just before it slides off the edge of my desk, and I give her a dirty look. "There's no way you can have read and written your own answers, Steph."

She grins. "I totally don't have time to do it all." She wiggles her eyebrows, grins at me, and begins coughing. "Work with me, Anne," she whispers and starts coughing some more. She gestures to me, pointing toward the whispering teachers while continuing to cough, and I groan under my breath.

Other students are beginning to look over at us—not that Steph cares, but I certainly do. I give Johnny, the guy I sometimes get teamed up with for calculus because he needs help constantly and the teacher is too lazy to spend the time showing him twenty times over how to do the sum, the middle finger and he chuckles and looks away.

I reluctantly raise my hand, attempting to interrupt Mr. Jeffreys, but he glances my way and chooses to ignore me. Looking back at Steph, though, she isn't giving up on her crappy plan. "Excuse me, sir?" I say after clearing my throat. He glances over at me, his conversation with Mrs. Marsh stalling. "Umm, Steph isn't feeling so good, can she go to the see the nurse?"

Mr. Jeffreys looks at Mrs. Marsh uncertainly before Steph pulls out all the punches and stands from her chair and coughs fitfully.

"Sir, I really don't feel too good," she whines pathetically.

Mrs. Marsh nods rapidly, going so far as to back up behind Mr. Jeffreys's desk as he agrees to let her out of class and Steph passes them by. I scrunch up my nose at the ridiculousness of it all, but curiosity gets the better of me.

"Sir? I think I should go with her," I say, standing up. I'm fifteen, and if I can get out of class, then I will.

"I think you should just sit down and get on with your work, young lady," he says with a huff, and I sit back in my chair. Johnny snickers and I scowl at him before opening my book back up.

Mrs. Marsh crouches down to Mr. Jeffreys's level and whispers something to him, their voices raising but not enough for me to make out what they're saying. They continue to whisper back and forth while I pretend I'm not listening to them.

"Anne, go see that Stephanie is okay."

I look up in confusion. Mr. Jeffreys is frowning so he's clearly not happy about letting me go, but I don't need to be told twice and I jump back up out of my seat, grab my bag, and dash out after Steph, making sure to shoot Johnny a wide grin as I go. Surprisingly he smiles back at me, and I can't stop the blush that rises to my cheeks.

I head to the nurse's station, following after Steph, even though I know she wouldn't actually go there, but needing to confirm my suspicion nonetheless. Why would she? She's not really sick and the nurse would see right through the façade. I walk past the door, looking in through the small crack, and as suspected, Steph isn't there, but the small room is busy. Plenty of kids are obviously trying to get out of class today. I snigger to myself and continue down the hallway, heading toward the bathroom—the more likely place she'll be.

I push the door open and see Steph talking to Amy Bell, a little bitchy girl that hangs around Steph like a fly on...well, she's a hanger-oner. And if she's hanging onto Steph, that means she's hanging onto me, and I can't stand her. She causes trouble wherever we go, and I don't want any more hassle from my parents. I groan, frowning at her, ignoring the scowl on her face. We've come to a stalemate in our triangular friendship, silently agreeing to ignore each other as much as possible. Because as much as Steph pisses me off, I do care about her. We've been friends since we were little kids, and though life is trying to take us in different directions, I refuse to lose my childhood friend just yet.

"Hey." I nod to them both and lean back against the sink, dropping my bag at my feet.

"What did Mr. Jeffreys say?" Steph grins.

I shrug. "Not much—he didn't seem too bothered. Something's going on though. Did you see the way Mrs. Marsh came in?" I bite the inside of my cheek, thinking about how panicked she had looked.

"She's a stuck up bitch, maybe her cat died," Amy says and they both laugh.

"No, it seems serious whatever it is. She was really panicked." Now I sound like the whiny one, sticking up for the school secretary. I turn and look at my reflection in the mirror. I have blond hair like Steph, but where hers is bright with natural honey streaks running through it, mine is more of a dull, mousy blond. Where her eyes are crystal blue, mine are a pale blue—almost gray. She's Barbie, and I'm Barbie's dull-looking sister.

The fire alarm goes off, making us all jump and laugh simultaneously. "We better go." I look back around at them, but Steph is shaking her head and I scowl at her. "You know the rules—we need to get to the tennis courts for the fire drill.

We don't have a choice about that, and no amount of coughing will get you out of it." I sling my bag over my shoulder and push on the bathroom door. "You coming?"

"No way. It's bullshit anyway," she snipes, looking at Amy with a grin. "Just a stupid fire drill."

"Fine, whatever." I push my way out into the hallway, ignoring Amy calling me a goody two-shoes with a laugh. I roll my eyes and make my way to the tennis courts to line up with everyone else. It may be just a fire drill, but the school tends to take them pretty seriously.

It's busy outside, every class getting into disorderly lines and being yelled at by panicked teachers, and I begin to worry that perhaps it's not a drill. I stand behind Dean, one of the brainboxes from a higher class than me. We're in the same year but his IQ is off the charts so we don't have any classes together. Not that I'm not clever; just that compared to Dean, most people look dumb—including the teachers.

It's hot and sticky standing around, but the fire alarm is still ringing; and as I look around seeing the panic on teachers' faces and the worried expressions of my classmates. I realize we're all beginning to think that maybe there is a real fire in the school. This wouldn't be a problem for anyone, including me, but I keep thinking of Steph and Amy hiding out in the girls' bathroom. I bite the inside of my cheek worrying about what to do, when Dean turns to me.

"There's something going down," he whispers.

"Yeah, I get that feeling too." I glance at the other lines of students, looking for Steph just in case she changed her mind.

"I was in trig when Mr. Hartley got a call on his cell," he says, watching me closely. I shrug and he continues. "He took that call, left the room, and didn't come back."

My pale blue eyes meet his dark brown ones. "He just…left?" I frown.

"Yup." Dean folds his arms over his chest and nods, seeming pleased that he actually got my attention.

The guy has fancied the pants off me since first grade, always following me around and trying to talk to me. He seems like a nice enough guy, but he's just not my type. Not that I have a type yet, but I know that whatever it is, it's not him. He's skinny and tall—lanky, almost—with hair that always looks scruffy and skin that always looks dirty. And he's clever, like ridiculously clever, and makes me feel like a dumbass every time I've ever spoken to him. I don't think he even knows he's doing it—or maybe he does and he gets off on making girls feel stupid.

Four yellow school buses speed into the school grounds and pull up to the front of the tennis courts. Our head teacher claps her hands to get our attention and all eyes fall on her as she speaks.

"Okay, children, we need to get everyone to the town hall immediately. Your parents will be waiting for you there. Move in an orderly fashion, no silliness and no arguments about it, we need to do this quickly." She turns tail and heads for the first bus without waiting to hear anyone out.

Slowly we begin to filter toward the buses, all mumbling and whispering our annoyance and confusion.

Dean looks over his shoulder at me. "I'm going to get my car. I'm not leaving it here, I saved up all summer for it. Do you want to ride with me? It'll be quicker." He smiles warmly.

"You won't get anywhere near the parking lot." I gesture around us at the teachers lining our way.

"Don't you worry your pretty little head about that, just follow me." He smirks.

I shake my head at him. "I'm not coming with you. Besides, you're going to get in a ton of shit when they see you at the town hall."

Dean frowns and then shrugs, looking both annoyed and disappointed that I'm not going to be riding in his car. "Suit yourself. You follow the lemmings, then." He takes off quickly, pushing past two teachers and out of the tennis courts. One makes to follow after him but then changes her mind after a couple of steps, ushering us forward quicker without even a second look back at Dean.

I sit on the bus and watch Dean's silver Prius peel out of the parking lot, and can't stop my grin. None of the teachers seem too concerned. In fact, when I think about it, none of them have even bothered to take roll call to make sure that we're all present. I frown and curse under my breath, realizing that Steph still isn't here. I raise my hand to let our student counselor know when she climbs aboard and the doors to the bus shut. But she dismisses me with a wave of her hand and sits down next to the driver.

As the buses finally pull away from school, leaving Steph and Amy behind, I worry—but then the bitchy part of me decides that it's their own damn fault for being such brats. Maybe it will teach Steph a lesson this time and she'll finally stay away from Amy. At least then I'll get my friend back all to myself. I glance back out the window, looking up at the windows on the school, and wonder if Steph and Amy are looking out and seeing us all leaving. I hope so; at least then they'll have the good sense to get in their cars and follow us.

Two.

The bus driver is driving too fast—way too fast. I know this because I've nearly fallen out of my seat three times, and I'm just glad that I'm sitting on my own and not sharing; otherwise I would have ended up in someone's lap, or vice versa. I grip the back of the seat in front of me tighter, feeling my backpack move on my shoulders as we swing around another corner. I suck in a breath and blink several times to clear my tears. I never liked going fast. My daddy always used to tease me when we had to go on the highway and I'd cry.

One of the guidance counselors is sitting up front with the driver, but she doesn't bother to tell him to slow down—in fact, almost like she wants him to go even faster, which makes my stomach does a little flip. I realize that my heart is thumping in my chest and I open my eyes and look around, seeing how worried all my classmates look, and feel glad that it's not just me. None of us are talking, not even muttering under our breath as the bus bumps down the road, rocking from side to side, and I wonder if we're all as clueless as to what's going on.

The only noise is the sound of the tires screeching and soft sobbing coming from somewhere near the back of the bus. I reach into my backpack with one hand and pull out my cell phone to call my parents. I haven't called before now because…well, up until now I didn't worry too much, and my parents never really care anyway. They're always so busy with work that a phone call to them has to be a major emergency or there's hell to pay for interrupting them when they're at work. Lord knows how they'll be when they have to come pick me up.

I flick the silent button off my cell phone as I pull it out and then stare at the screen in shock for a moment. There's seven missed calls from my parents' number. Seven. That's unheard of from them. I don't think they've ever called me seven times in my *life*, never mind in one day. I press the call back button and put the phone to my ear with shaky hands, but it beeps and cuts out. I try again and get the same reply. I slip my phone back into my bag in frustration and chew on the inside of my cheek again—hard enough to draw blood this time, but I don't care. I barely register the little nick of pain in my mouth. Worry is set deep in my bones now, because for my parents to call me things must be bad. Really bad.

For the hundredth time I think of Steph and Amy, cursing them both for being such spoiled little bitches. Yet no matter how pissed I am at Steph, I know I have to tell someone that she's still back at school, or at least try. I huff and stand up, carefully making my way to the front of the bus. I tap our guidance counselor's shoulder, and she turns with a small squeal, her face blanching. Or perhaps it was blanched already. Her eyes are rimmed red, black mascara streaked down her puffy cheeks, and she does nothing to hide any of this, like a good counselor should do.

"What is it, Anne? What do you want?" she snaps.

"I need to tell you something," I mumble, shocked at being shouted at by her. She's normally so nice and calming, not this wreck of a woman in front of me.

She stands up and shoos me away. "Go back to your seat immediately, Anne, this is not the time for teenage drama!"

I stare at her, my mouth opening and closing as if words were coming out, but none are. She shoos me again and sits back down. I turn and head back to my seat, looking at my classmates and expecting to see them smirking or laughing at me for getting yelled at, but none are; they all look as equally frightened as I now feel.

I steady myself by holding onto the backs of the seats as I stumble back to sit down again. The bus turns too sharply, and I hear the driver cuss loudly before we hit something with a thud. Everyone aboard the bus screams, including me, and I cling onto a seat to stop myself from falling over. The bus tires screech loudly as we keep on going, ignoring the accident we just caused and the fact that we're all scared half to death. The crying is louder now, and I turn to look out the front window of the bus, seeing smoke rising from the engine and blood splatter on the window.

I swallow down the lump in my throat, fear and panic gripping me tightly. The bus goes around another corner, but it's still going too quickly despite the fact that we just hit someone or something, and I feel the tires on one side of the bus leave the ground. It leans to one side, and despite how hard I hold onto the back of a seat, as the bus flips onto its side I end up sprawling across the floor. Bags and students land on top of me, and I tuck in my legs and wrap my arms over my head to protect myself as the sound of screeching metal and glass smashing almost drowns out the sound of screams all around me.

My body hits a window, and I feel it crack underneath my weight. Something hard hits my side and I groan and try to push it off me as the bus continues to roll before finally coming to a stop. Everything falls silent, barring the ticking of the engine and the intermittent sobbing coming from somewhere. I close my eyes, feeling a warm trickle of blood slide between my breasts. I open my eyes and look down, and see a long shard of glass sticking into my chest. It doesn't seem too deep, thankfully, but it hurts and it's bleeding badly.

I push away the bags that have landed on me and stumble up to standing. My backpack is still on, and I'm thankful when I see all the broken glass underneath me that would have cut into my back if I hadn't been wearing it. I grip the glass shard sticking between my breasts and pull with a sharp squeal. A fresh burst of blood escapes and I press the palm of my hand to it to stop the flow, tears springing in my eyes at the pain.

I can still hear crying, but the bus is a tangled mess of bodies, backpacks, and torn metal, and I still can't see where it's coming from. I step over a prone body, trying not to look at who it is, my hand still pressed against my chest. I walk the center aisle—or what is now the center aisle but used to be the side of the bus—and try to avoid standing on the broken windows as best I can. I can't see any student with their eyes open—certainly none that look alive—and I let out the sob that I've been holding onto.

My vision swims and I clutch the side of a seat to steady myself until the vertigo stops, and then I keep moving toward the front of the bus. The front window is completely blown out, the bus driver having gone through it, and I look out and see his mangled body on the asphalt. Blood is pooling around him, and I can tell even from this distance that his skull is disfigured and broken and I sob loudly again, not even trying to contain my crying.

I climb out the window, small fragments of glass digging into the palms of my hands, and slide down the hood of the bus. I land on my feet but stumble onto my ass, momentarily letting go of my chest and releasing a fresh burst of blood from the wound. Steam is pouring from the front of the bus, a hissing and ticking as if it is tired and weary after a long day on the road, and I drag myself away from it as quickly as I can.

I look back up the road, expecting to see police cars or ambulances, fire trucks, or at the very least the other school buses, but there are none. I reach behind me into my backpack and fumble around for my cell, my fingers finally grasping it. I press the call button and hold it to my ear but there's no sound, no dial tone, nothing. I clutch it in my hand, my chin trembling, and look up the road when I hear a sound. I can see people coming toward the wreck, and I barely contain my cry of relief that someone is coming to help.

I close my eyes tightly, barely controlling the tears that want to explode from me, and keep my hand pressed to my chest. My chin quivers, my body trembling as I slink into what must be shock. I need to be strong. Help will be here soon and then I can go to the hospital. My parents will meet me there and this will all be over.

Tires screech to a halt in front of me and I open my eyes. Dean is climbing out of his Prius, his face contorted in worry as he looks at me. He glances back to the approaching people and then to me, keeping his distance until I reach a hand out to him.

"I need help. The bus…crashed. I got glass," I point down at my chest, and his eyes follow, widening as he sees all the blood.

"You're not bitten?"

I frown at him. "What? No. Why would I be bitten?"

He moves toward me quickly. "We need to go now, Anne."

He reaches down and loops his arm around my waist, pulling me up to him. Even in my current state of pain and confusion, I feel him pulling me unnecessarily close to his body. I look into his face, his worry evident, but his eyes wash over me with something more. I don't have time to consider what, though, as he half-drags, half-carries me around to the passenger side of his car and sets me in it.

"I need to get to the hospital," I murmur painfully, my head swimming and my stomach feeling nauseous now that I've moved.

"No chance of that anytime soon," he says and slams my door.

I frown, wondering what he means, but I feel dizzy and sick and can't think about anything but the pain in my head and chest right now.

I hear a yell and look out my window, seeing Dean talking to our guidance counselor, and breathe a sigh of relief that someone else made it out of the crash alive. I rest my head back on the seat and close my eyes, hoping the dizziness will pass before Dean takes me to a hospital. I think I might hurl if he tries to drive me anywhere at the moment.

A loud thud and crack make me open my eyes and I look out my window to see Dean swinging a baseball bat against the ground. I lean forward, my nose pressed against the glass to look out of my window, and a startled yell leaves my mouth before I can stop it. Dean looks up to me with a scowl and then swings the bat against our counselor's head again. The last smash does it and blood explodes from out of her ears. Her hands, which were reaching for him, flop to the ground and she stops flailing, only an occasional twitch to her fingers. I scream again.

Dean pants heavily and then looks back up to the wreckage. His eyes go wide and he jogs around to the driver's side of the car. I want to lock the door and keep him out, keep him away from me. He's clearly unhinged, but right at that moment all I can do is lean forward and hurl all over the foot well of his car. I hear him climb inside and start the engine as I gag and retch, images of Dean smashing in our counselor's head intruding on my thoughts wherever they stray. I sob loudly, blood and snot mixing, and I look across at Dean as he begins to drive.

"Where are you taking me?" I cry out, my chin trembling. "Please don't hurt me."

He glances across at me, his eyes cold. "Somewhere safe. I'm going to protect you." He returns his eyes to the road and I let the silence pass.

Protect me? Protect me from what? I sob again, crying loudly. Every wracking sob sends pain shooting through my chest, and when I look down I see that blood is seeping through my fingers. I look back up to him and see that he's watching me.

"The blood will attract them, we need to stop it quickly," Dean says darkly.

He pulls the car over to the side of the road and reaches under his seat. I flinch as he pulls out something and leans toward me, my eyes squeezing tightly shut.

"Don't hurt me." I cower away from him.

I hear a click, but when nothing happens I open my eyes and see him staring at me with a frown. "I'm not going to hurt you. I need to cover the injury." He holds up some gauze and bandages. "Take off your top."

I shake my head and he tuts.

"Now is not the time to be a prude. I need to stop the bleeding, Anne, now take off your top!" he yells, but I still shake my head.

Dean leans over and yanks the straps of my top down my arms. I fight him with one hand even as he cusses at me. His hand draws back and he slaps me hard across the cheek and I feel the sting of it right down to my toes. I scream out at him to stop, but his hand goes to my throat, pressing me back against my door.

"I need to stop the bleeding, nothing else, now calm down," he says through gritted teeth. "I'm not going to hurt you." He glances at my cheek, to what I suspect must be a bright red slap mark, and to his credit he looks guilty about it.

My chin trembles but I stop fighting him, letting him pull my straps down my arms so he can look at the cut between my breasts. He slowly pulls my hand away and looks at it before rooting through his first aid box again and pulling out some tape. He looks back up into my face, his eyes looking at my cheek again.

"I'm sorry about that, I didn't mean to hurt you. I know this is scary for you." He pours some liquid onto some gauze and slowly pries my hand away, swapping it for the gauze. It stings and I hiss painfully, and he looks shameful that he hurt me.

"What's going on? Where are you taking me?" I say my voice almost a whisper in the confined space.

Dean looks up into my eyes, a frown puckering between his eyebrows. "You have to be strong now and listen to me carefully. I'm going to protect you."

I don't say anything, and I don't object when he swaps one soaked cotton ball for another.

He continues. "The apocalypse has started. I'm going to take us somewhere safe."

He swaps the ball for some gauze, taping it over the wound, and then pulls me forward so he can wrap a bandage around it all. It hurts and burns and I hiss again, but my thoughts aren't on my wound, they're on what he just said, and how far into insanity he must have fallen.

"The apocalypse?" I snort incredulously. He only nods and continues checking that the tape is tight enough over my wound.

"But we're going to be all right, Anne. Don't worry about anything, I have everything under control." He doesn't smile but a light is in his eyes, as if he's been waiting for this moment his whole life.

Three.

We drive into town, avoiding crashed cars and homes that are ablaze. The worst horror though, is the people we narrowly avoid hitting with the car. They stumble into our path, arms raised and teeth snapping as if possessed by the devil. I press a hand to my mouth to stop the scream escaping from my throat as I watch the horror unfolding. Nothing could have prepared me for this. Not Dean's words. Nothing. I look across at him sharply, his jaw twitching as he grinds his teeth.

"How did you know what was going on?"

He swerves around another person with expertise. "I was watching the news this morning, there have been reports for days of some new outbreak all over the country, but today it seemed to reach a whole new level." He glances across at me. "They said that they were shutting down hospitals and not accepting any new patients, that people had to stay at home."

"I heard no such thing!" I snap. "You're making this up."

He shakes his head. "This was across state. It stood to reason that whatever this is was going to spread here. When all you lemmings got on the school bus, I drove my car into town and saw," he gestures around us, "this." He seems almost apologetic as he says it, as if this was all his fault.

"So, what now? We need to get to the town hall—my parents are there waiting for me." I realize that I've dropped my phone into the pool of vomit at my feet and I grimace.

Dean looks across at me with a frown. "No one is coming out of there," he says, and slows the car as we pass the town hall. Blood covers the steps leading up into the building, bodies litter the open doorway, and smoke is pouring through one of the lower windows.

"My parents!" I cry, tears breaking free of my eyes again. "I need to go and see if they're there."

"They're gone, Anne."

I scowl at Dean. "I need to go see, this can't be happening."

"You're not going in there, you'll get yourself killed!"

"Let me out of this damn car right now."

Dean shakes his head and looks back at the town hall. I grab the handle of the door and dive out. The car is only going slow, but man it hurts when my shoulder hits the ground, my body rolling unapologetically. My head cracks against the hard ground and sends stars into my vision, and I groan loudly.

I hear Dean slam on his brakes and yell my name, but I force myself to stand even as the world continues to spin, and I jog in the direction of the town hall. My equilibrium must be completely off because I can't seem to run in a straight line; instead, my body wants to go left, so it doesn't take long for Dean to catch up and tackle me back to the ground.

"Get off me!" I yell at him, but he doesn't; he grabs me by the back of my sweater and drags me to my feet, pulling me back toward the car. "I said get off me," I yell again.

"You're going to get us both killed, now shut the hell up," he yells.

Dean pushes me back inside the car and clicks my belt in place before slamming the door shut. He watches me through the window, obviously knowing that as soon as he makes a move for the driver's side I'm going to make a run for it again. He looks back at the town hall, and his face pales. I reluctantly follow Dean's gaze, my chin beginning to tremble again as I watch bloodied people stumbling out the door of the town hall. I don't recognize any of them, but then I'm not sure if I even would since they don't resemble anything human anymore.

People are bloodied from head to toe, limbs dangling uselessly or missing completely. Gaping holes cover their arms and faces, as if they've been attacked by wild animals. I finally see someone I recognize—Steph's mom. And I begin to cry silently, tears spilling down my cheeks. She drags herself out of the doorway by her arms, pulling her body behind her. Some of the other people follow her out, walking over her back and tripping over her head, but they don't care and she doesn't care. None of them seem to notice as she puts her nose to the air and looks like she's sniffing.

The driver's side doors opens and Dean climbs in. His hand touches the bottom of my chin, his fingers rubbing away some of my salty tears. I look away from the abomination that is Steph's mom and into his eyes.

"I told you, I'm going to protect you. We're going to be all right. Okay?" His other hand reaches over and he cups my face in his hands, keeping my attention on him. "Okay?" he repeats.

I nod, more tears spilling down my cheeks. Dean's eyes flit to my mouth and then back up into my eyes, and for a moment I think he might kiss me. A shudder runs through him, and he briefly closes his eyes and then opens them back up, a small smile on his mouth. And I briefly wonder what I've gotten myself into.

"Dean?" I whisper, wanting to pull away from him.

"Yes, Anne," he says almost breathlessly.

I nod toward his window, and he reluctantly tears his eyes from mine and follows my gaze. The people are stumbling toward the car, and they look…Angry? Hungry? Possessed? I don't know how to describe them, but they definitely don't look friendly.

"Shit!" Dean curses and lets go of my face.

I silently feel relief as he moves away from me, but don't dare voice it. Right now I need him. I need him to protect me and keep me safe until I can find my parents or the army or something comes into town to sort all this mess out. I would not survive out there on my own; I'm not stupid. I watch the side of his face as he slips the car into gear and we squeal away. I need him, and he wants me. I don't know what is worse, or what else there is to fear. He's just a high school boy and those things outside the window are...whatever they are. Monsters? Surely they're scarier than him?

"Where are we going?" I ask quietly. The pain in my chest is bad, but the pain behind my eyes is worse. I feel like I'm hungover, like the time I drank my dad's liquor. The pain is an incessant thudding inside my skull, as if there's too much pressure in there. I close my eyes and squeeze the bridge of my nose tightly in the hopes of relieving the pain.

"I'm taking you to my grandpa's house," he says matter-of-factly. "Everyone in our family used to call him crazy, but not me. He was a prepper of sorts—he'll have all different systems in place for this," he lets his words trail off, and I know that he wants to say apocalypse or end of days, or something equally as frightening.

I nod and rest my head on the seat back. My heart is still hammering, my chest still burning, and my head still pounding. I take a couple of deep breaths, the smell of my earlier vomit reaching my nose and making me gag.

"I'm sorry about the puke," I mumble, feeling embarrassed.

Dean chuckles. "That's okay. We'll hose it out when we get there."

We drive in silence for a while. I still feel the car swerving around what I presume to be the monsters roaming

116

the streets or perhaps car wrecks, but I don't have the energy to open my eyes back up. The stress and pain of the day is taking its toll on me, and while there's no chance of me sleeping anytime soon, I decide keeping my eyes closed to avoid the nightmares is a better option than keeping them open.

The car eventually slows, the ride becoming bumpy, and I force my eyes to open. Dean stops the car and climbs out, looking at the large house in front of us. It's a Victorian style with a sloping pointy red roof and a large awning all the way around it. A small swinging bench hangs on the porch, with a black cat sitting upon it. I decide I can't stay in the car with the smell of vomit any longer and I open the door and climb out, moving around the front of the car to stand with Dean.

His hand moves over, his fingers brushing against mine, but I move and fold my arms over my chest. He tuts and looks away.

"This isn't good," Dean says.

I look at him. "Why? What do you mean, it's not good?" I look around us and thankfully don't see anything or anyone else.

"Because if Gramps was in there he would be out here pointing a twelve-gauge at us by now," Dean says.

"Well surely that's a good thing. That he's not trying to blow off our heads."

Dean shakes his head and looks down at his shoes. "Nope, that was how he always greeted visitors. The fact that he isn't out here doing that very thing means he's dead."

Four.

I look at the front porch and then to Dean, feeling guilty for some strange reason. I shouldn't—I mean, this has nothing to do with me—but I do all the same.

"Should we go in there?" I say, looking back the way we just came in case any of those—people just followed us.

Dean shakes his head again and shrugs. "I guess, but I don't really want to."

I nod. "Oh." My mouth is dry—arid, really—the taste of stale vomit lingering in the back of my throat. "Do you have any water in your car?" I ask quietly. Feeling guilty again. This time for cutting into the silence and his grief.

Dean huffs—not an impatient huff, more of a tired, disappointed huff. Like a man coming home from work and realizing that he still has yard work to do.

"No, but we can get you something to drink inside." He walks around to the car, leans in, and pulls out his baseball bat. Then he takes my hand in his and leads me up the front steps.

I trail behind him, not really wanting to go inside but not wanting to stay out here, either. Nowhere seems safe right now. Not school, not the town hall—not even town itself. I think of Steph's mom and have to stop to bend over and catch my breath. Dean looks back at me but doesn't comment. His gray eyes watch my every move until I finally stand back up and nod that I'm okay to go.

He lets go of my hand to open the door, looking back once at me with a finger to his lips. Satisfied that I'm going to be quiet, he turns the handle, letting the door open slowly. The stale stench of something wafts out to us and I grimace as we step inside. We stop on the threshold, listening for any signs of movements. Moments pass by, but silence is the only thing that greets us. I clear my throat as quietly as I can as the incessant burning in my throat continues. Dean glances back again and then drags me through the house and into a large maple wood kitchen.

He grabs a glass that sits on the draining board and fills it at the sink before handing it to me. I take it from him and swallow it greedily, not even caring when the water splashes down my face. I swallow until the burning stops and it's less painful and more annoying. I look up at him with a huge smile, feeling insanely grateful. He leans back against the sink, the window behind him giving a great view of the yard and fields surrounding.

"Thank you." I lick my lips and smile again, my thirst finally feeling quenched.

We look at each other, getting lost in each other's confused expressions before a slow smile creeps up Dean's face, and he blushes and looks away. I hadn't meant the moment to become so intimate, yet it felt that way.

"So, what now?" I ask.

He looks back at me. "We clear this place, make it secure, and hunker down until everything sorts itself out. I guess." He shrugs like it's the most normal thing in the world and I nod in agreement, feeling surprisingly calm. My smile falters and then slips away completely as I stare behind Dean. He must sense that something isn't right, because he turns to look out of the window and curses. His shoulders slump as he grips the edge of the sink.

A man? God, can I even call it that? Because this thing is so far removed from being a man anymore. It walks slowly, its arms hanging limply by its sides, its shirt torn open wide, flapping in the slight breeze, and showing the world the wound that should be hidden underneath. The man-thing is missing

119

half its hair and missing a part of its cheek, as if the hair was ripped from his scalp pulling away flesh and tissue as well as graying hair.

"Grandpa," Dean mutters.

I place a hand on his shoulder and squeeze. "I'm so sorry."

Dean turns, wrapping his arms around my body and holding me tightly. I let him lean into me, his body melding to mine, and though it's uncomfortable, I let him. Because I can't imagine the horror of what he must be going through right now. Seeing a family member…like that must be the most horrifying thing ever. I pat his back, and slowly as I get more comfortable with his proximity I rub it gently, attempting to sooth him as I hush gently in his ear.

He eventually relents and pulls out of our embrace, looking into my face with a deep-seated sadness. His hands stay on my arms, as if he's afraid that I'll leave him; but I won't, of course. Where would I even go?

"What now?" I ask again, a repeat of my earlier question. Because things have changed now. We won't be safe with his decomposing grandpa stumbling around the property, but how do you suggest to someone they put their family member out of their misery?

Dean looks away from me, his hands still wrapped around my forearm. He breathes out a heavy breath. "I'll take care of it." He watches me to see if I'm happy about his decision. "I'll take care of him," he says to clarify, but he didn't need to. I knew what he meant.

"Okay," is all I can squeeze out of my too-tight throat.

He reaches for his baseball bat from the counter and leaves the kitchen without another word. I stare out the window, trying to see if there are any more of those…things, but I can't see any. It all seems too peaceful and ideal with him out of the show, and I find myself humming as I pour myself another glass of water.

Minutes pass, and as I begin to worry I hear the telltale thud of something—most likely Dean's bat hitting his grandpa's skull. I wince as I hear the sound again and again, and just when I think I can't bear it anymore it stops. I lean over the sink panting as my mouth fills with water and the urge to puke again is almost unbearable. A hand touches my shoulder and I let out a small squeal and flinch.

"It's okay." Dean's voice is deep and dark as he whispers, his words vibrating against my neck. I don't even feel any guilt when tears leak from my eyes. It was his grandpa, not mine, yet I'm the one crying. God, what is wrong with me?

I turn around, coming face to face with Dean. He's closer than I expected him to be. His arms are on either side of me, and he looks down into my face. His eyes flit to my lips and then back to my eyes, and I can sense his urge to kiss me. I clear my throat, place a hand on his chest, and push him back gently, putting some distance between us.

"Are you okay?" I ask, clearing my throat again.

He leans back on the opposite counter, resting on one elbow. "Yeah. Put him out of his misery." He shrugs like it's nothing.

"What's going on, Dean? I was sitting in my literature class just over two hours ago, and now my classmates are dead and the world is full of zombies. I don't understand any of this." I drag a hand down my face and bite the inside of my cheek, wincing at the cut I had made from my earlier gnawing.

Dean takes a deep breath before talking. "I told you, it's the apocalypse."

"But what does that mean?"

"It means that everything you've known up to this point is over. Life will never be the same again." He stuffs his hands into his front pockets and looks me head-on. "It's just you and me against the world now, but I told you—I'll protect you, you don't need to worry." He smiles shyly, but it does nothing to calm me down.

"Dean, it's not about keeping me safe, this," I gesture around us, meaning not just the unfamiliar house that I've found myself in but the world, "is crazy! The whole world has gone freaking crazy. What about my family and my friends? Are they all dead? Oh my God, this can't be happening."

Dean walks toward me, placing his hands on my biceps and looks down into my face. "It's going to be okay."

"Is it?" I say, my voice almost a screech.

He pulls me against his chest and I wrap my arms around his middle, holding him close while I cry. "This is just, I don't even…" I can't form a cohesive thought as I cry. "Steph is still at school." I pull back from him and he reluctantly lets me go. "Her and Amy were hiding out in the bathroom, they said it was probably just a fire drill."

"So?" Dean frowns.

"So? They could be alive, they could need our help!" I push away from him, wiping away the tears and snot with my sleeve. "We need to go get them."

"We can't go back out there, Anne. That's suicide." Dean says it so matter-of-factly, like it's the most absurd thing to even think about going.

"I need to see if my parents are okay, Dean. You understand that, right? I mean, they could be okay. We don't know that everyone is dead." I drag my hand down my face again, undoubtedly smearing my mascara, but I don't care, for once I just don't care. "What about your parents?"

Dean snorts out his contempt. "I don't know, and I don't care."

I don't ask any questions; it's his life, his drama. Right now I have enough of my own.

"Why do you even care about yours? They never give a shit over you," he says while pacing the kitchen, anxiety rolling off him in waves.

"How do you know that? You don't know anything about me," I spit out, feeling more annoyed by the second. So what if he's right, that I know I'm more of a hindrance to my parents than anything else? That most nights I eat alone, and we barely speak to one another anymore. So what that if I've been looking forward to leaving home for as far back as I can remember? So the hell what? I stare at Dean, all my anger and annoyance pouring into the glower.

"It's obvious, Anne. You think people don't see you, that people don't care, but we do—I do." He points to himself and continues. "I see how your parents never come to any school meetings or shows, how you're always alone, how most of the time when anyone walks by with their parents you look away, like you can't bear to see anyone else's happy family. And I'm telling you that I get it, I'm in the same boat." It's his turn to sound dramatic and high-pitched now. He continues to pace the kitchen, his arms flailing around him. He stops and looks at me, his anger quickly leaving him when he sees the effect his words have on me. "I just want you to know that I see you, I'm here for you, and we're going to be okay." His voice cracks on his words, and that's all it takes to make my tears spill down my cheeks again.

He comes toward me quickly, wrapping his arms around my body and pressing my face back into his chest like we had been not five minutes before. He's right, I know he's right, yet I just can't seem to let go of them—my parents. The sad part is, I know that if they were somewhere safe, they wouldn't put themselves at risk to come. They'd just see me as an expendable loss.

I sob louder and make a decision, one that will probably haunt me for the rest of my life—however short or long that may be right now. I pull out of the embrace and look up into his face, seeing not just the annoying, gangly kid that I've grown up with, but someone who is being the man in this terrible situation and who is clearly going to do whatever it takes to keep me safe. I can't turn down that gift, that friendship. I need him way more than he needs me.

I take a shuddering breath. "Okay, so we stay here. Clear the house, do what we can to keep safe until everything…blows over?"

He looks at me firmly and nods. "That's my girl."

I don't know when I became *his* girl, but I don't have the emotional ability to argue with him right now. Instead I give him a small smile.

"Okay, so, what do we do first?" I ask.

"Grandpa had a storm shelter. I suggest we check that out, see how safe it is, and what provisions he has. Then I guess we need to gather weapons, water, and food, in that order." Dean scrubs at his chin, scratching at the small amount of hair he has growing there. "Do you want to stay here while I go check everything out?"

I shake my head frantically. "Hell no, I'm coming with you."

He smiles and takes my hand and leads me out of the kitchen and down the hall. At the end of the hallway is a wooden door. It looks like a cloakroom of some kind, but when he opens the door another door is in there. This one looks to be a sturdy metal, with several locks on the outside.

"Shit," Dean mumbles.

I look at him quizzically.

"Grandpa probably has the keys on him. Crazy old coot never trusted nobody."

I grimace, knowing how hard this is going to be on him—having to rifle through his dead grandpa's pockets. The same grandpa that he just beat to death with a baseball bat.

"Do you want me to do it?" I ask, hoping that he doesn't agree to this, but knowing that I should at least offer. After all, he's done so much for me.

"Do what?"

"Look through his pockets for the keys."

Dean barks out a laugh. "Let a girl help? No, I can handle this." He pats me on the shoulder condescendingly. "I'll be right back." He turns on his heel and leaves through the front door.

I'm too stunned by his sexist attitude to say anything until after he's gone. "Stupid high school boys!" I yell after him and stamp my foot, and I swear I hear him laugh.

A bang from upstairs makes me jump, but thankfully I refrain from screaming and living up to Dean's obviously low standard of women in scary situations. I grab an umbrella from the coat stand—one with a sharp silver point on the end—and creep up the stairs. My steps are almost silent, and if my heart weren't ready to beat out of my chest I'd be pretty impressed by my stealth skills. But the situation as it is means that I actually feel like vomiting in fear as I hear the noise again. Like a dull thud and scrape sound. I shudder as my imagination runs wild. But I have to do this. I have to prove to that asshole that I can handle myself, that I'm not a total girl in these situations.

I reach the top of the stairs and come to several closed doors. I stop and listen, waiting to hear the noise again, and when I hear it I continue quietly until I'm standing outside one of the closed doors—one which I assume is the bedroom, but of course can't be certain.

I grip the umbrella tighter and take a deep breath as I open it.

Five.

The door opens quietly, no horror movie creak or anything jumping out on me, but that doesn't stop me from wanting to pee myself. I peer around the room and hear movement from the small bathroom in the corner.

I let out my breath slowly and slide myself along the wall until I reach the doorway, keeping my umbrella/badass-zombie-killing-weapon as close to my chest as possible and ready to be wielded at a moment's notice. I peer around the doorway and see someone moving by the window. A man, boy, I'm not sure, but from the back they seem male. There's blood on the floor and across their back, and I know it must be one of the monsters from earlier.

I bit down on the inside of my cheek, raise my deadly weapon up, and charge into the room with all intent of slamming it through the back of this monster's skull. At the last possible moment he turns and stares at me with wide eyes and lets out a scream—a scream! —which in turn makes me scream. I hear pounding coming up the stairs and Dean charges into the room with his baseball bat raised, while me and whoever the heck this other guy is stand there screaming at each other.

"Malcolm?" Dean yells above the noise we're making.

The guy I presume to be Malcolm stops screaming, and so do I. His mouth turns up into a handsome smile. "Dean? You're okay?"

The two guys charge each other, wrapping their arms around one another in a manly embrace and leave me feeling stupid and with a very sore throat. They eventually pull out of the embrace to look at me.

"What's this chick's problem? She tried to beat me with an umbrella." Malcolm laughs, but he holds a hand out to show his friendliness. "I'm Malcolm, Dean's older cousin."

I take it with a scowl.

"I'm—"

"This is Anne," Dean interrupts, putting an arm across my shoulder defensively. "And you're barely older than me, smart-ass."

"Oh, sorry, bro." Malcolm smiles at me and then Dean, and Dean pulls me closer to his side. "So, did you see Grandpa yet?" Malcolm says more seriously, and I don't even have time to correct either boy and let them know that I'm not *with* Dean.

I pull away from Dean, keeping my umbrella clutched to my chest, and scowl at him. "Did you get the keys?" I ask.

"Yeah, I saw Grandpa. I took care of him." He turns to look at me. "And yeah, I got the keys."

Malcolm rubs the hair on his chin as he talks. He has a definite bad boy persona coming from him, and I wonder why I've never seen him in school before. I let my gaze travel over him, mentally comparing both him and Dean, and then flush in embarrassment that I'm even looking at Malcolm in that way. The world just ended and I'm eyeing up potential boyfriend material. I am such a slut—or that's what Steph would have said.

"The old bastard tried to eat me." Malcolm laughs and pulls out some cigarettes. "I came to check that he was okay, what with all the crazy going on, and he chased me around the damn house. I had to kick the dog out into the yard to give him something to chase instead of me." He laughs, but I can see it's just an act.

"Trixie?" Dean asks with sadness tingeing his voice.

"Yeah, I think she got away but I was too busy trying to find where he kept his guns to watch for too long. Stupid thing

128

kept yapping at the back door to be let back in, but I haven't seen her for some time now." He lights his cigarette and takes a drag. "Aaah, well, at least we can get the hell out of here now, right?"

Dean takes my hand and leads me down the stairs, and Malcolm follows closely behind. When I look back Malcolm is watching me with a smile that I reciprocate. We stop in front of the metal door and Dean relents my hand so that he can unlock it and let us all inside. He reaches back to take my hand in his once he finds the light switch but I pretend that I don't see it and push past him into the room. I don't want to keep giving him mixed messages, or Malcolm.

The room actually consists of several small rooms, much like a house underneath a house. With a bathroom, kitchen, bedroom, and living area. There's also a large storage area that's plenty stocked with canned food, bottled water, blankets, and weapons.

"Holy crap!" I whisper, my eyes bugging from me. "We could last here for ages," I say, finally smiling.

"Yeah, I guess Grandpa wasn't so crazy after all," Malcolm says.

I turn to look at him, my cheeks flush in excitement from knowing that we can survive here relatively comfortably for a long while. And with two men around for protection, I know that we're going to be fine. Malcolm finishes his cigarette and stubs it out on the concrete floor and I frown at which he grins and picks up the butt.

"Sorry, old habits," he says and stashes the butt in his pocket. "I can't believe he's been stashing all this stuff. I thought maybe he had a couple of guns, but this is insane. A good insane though." He chuckles and lets his eyes bore into mine.

Dean wraps his arm around my shoulder again. "See, I told you I'd look after you." He gestures around him, but for the first time since he helped me at the side of the road, I don't feel protected. His look has a glint of crazy in it, and the weight of his arm on me makes me want to shudder.

I slink out from under his grasp with a smile, not wanting to upset him and be kicked out, but again, not wanting to give the wrong impression. "You did. And we will all definitely be okay here."

He doesn't say anything to me, his smile falling from his face as he looks from me to Malcolm and back again, and then he walks back up the stairs without saying a word. I shudder now—flat-out, full-on shudder. Because him not saying anything is way creepier than him actually voicing his thoughts. At least that I could argue with, but God knows what's going through that mind of his. I look to Malcolm for a little help or reassurance but he just shrugs and walks back up the stairs also, leaving me alone in this fake little house below a house.

I wonder if I've just got into bed with the devil to protect myself, or if I ever had a choice to begin with.

Six.

"Water's running low again," I say to Dean as I lean out the front door.

He gets up from the swinging chair on the porch with a heavy sigh. "I'm on it."

He leaves his spot and marches down the three small steps and over to the small barn area. Inside we've set up a water collective tank. Actually, it's another thing that his grandpa had thought of in the event of some crazy emergency like this. It's a unit that collects the rainwater from the outside and funnels it inside to a purifying tank. The water is cleaned and made safe to drink again. It's supposed to work on all water, including toilets, etc., but we aren't that desperate yet. Yet.

The only pain to this is getting the water to the house, since his grandpa set it up in the large shed. I can only think that there had to be a little crazy to go with his brilliance.

Malcolm comes out of the house behind me and offers me a cup of coffee. It's funny how I never really liked the stuff until the apocalypse. I think it's more the smell than anything else. It reminds me of Mom and Dad. They always made a fresh percolator-full every morning, and the smell was what I woke up to. Somehow, drinking it makes me feel less homesick. Which I know is ridiculous because my home life was anything but great, but still. It was my home life, and now it's gone.

We've been at the house for almost three weeks, and only once ventured close to town. The place was a mess of dead and undead, and we haven't been back since. We check the radio every night for any news from the government, but so far nothing. Every once in a while one of the sick people comes across our property and Dean or Malcolm puts them out of their misery.

I can tell that Dean isn't happy about it though. He doesn't like killing the people, but he does it for me, to make me feel safe. I know I should feel bad about that, because he's going against his own morals because of his feelings for me—feelings which are not reciprocated—but I don't feel bad. I just feel happy that they're taking care of business and I don't have to get my hands dirty. I'm just glad to be safe.

Malcolm is different altogether. He doesn't care about the killing. Some would say he relishes in it. And he's good at it too. In fact, both boys are fully capable with both close proximity kills and gun use—though they try to not use the guns unless absolutely necessary. Who knew that Dean, the brainbox of our high school, would be so good at killing?

I take a sip of the coffee, breathing in its smell, and close my eyes so I can picture Mom and Dad's faces. In my head they're happy and healthy, and of course alive. This disease, infection, whatever it is, came from nowhere. I vaguely remember seeing some news reports on it up until the day of the outbreak in our small part of the world, but I never paid much notice, if I'm honest. You never think these things will actually affect you.

It seemed to hit everywhere at once, as if it was already living inside each of us, incubated and ready to be born. And this thing spreads quickly, from what I remember. Hell, from what I saw happen to our town, I can vouch for that. We still can't be sure what spreads it. Is it a bite? Direct saliva or blood transference? We know one thing for a hundred percent certainty: death brings death. All three of us have agreed to put each other out of our misery if it happens to us.

"It's been pretty quiet for a couple of days, huh?" Malcolm says.

"Yeah, I guess." I look out to the horizon. The sun is beginning to set, casting a beautiful orange glow across the field to the back of the property. To the front we have a couple of vehicles, Dean's Prius, Malcolm's motorbike, Grandpa's truck, and a beat-up red Ford. We found that one abandoned on the road leading up to the house a week back. No one was inside, and all the doors were open. There were bags of clothes and some boxes of food and water, and as much as I felt bad that we took it, deep down I know that the people who were driving that car were dead now.

Malcolm's hand touches my waist tentatively and I look back over my shoulder at him. He licks his lips and offers me a shy smile.

"Not here, he'll see," I whisper nervously, watching as Dean pulls the cart full of water back.

"I don't see what the problem is if he does," Malcolm huffs.

"Because he's very...*protective* of me, and I do not want to leave here," I snap.

"He's going to find out sooner or later."

"Let's make sure it's later rather than sooner then." I glance at him. "Go help him with the water, please," I add on the end, giving him a smile and hoping that Dean doesn't see it.

"Fine," Malcolm says and hands me his cup.

He jogs down the steps toward Dean, and I turn to go back inside. Back in the little kitchen, I search the cupboards for what we will be eating for our supper tonight. It's funny how quickly you miss the little things like fresh fruit and vegetables. And TV. God, I miss watching TV. I miss watching *America's Next Top Model*, and often find myself daydreaming about who would have won in the end.

I hear the boys coming back into the house and pulling the large cart of water into the kitchen. They put it into the corner of the room and begin filling the empty water containers with it.

"What's for dinner?" Dean asks, coming around the counter.

He smiles at me warmly as he comes up behind me to look over my shoulder and into the cupboard. His face is close to mine and I hear him take a deep breath as if breathing me in. I step away from him and move to another cupboard.

"I, uh, thought we could have soup," I say, grabbing the first can I see.

Dean smiles again. "That sounds lovely. Anything I can do to help?"

He moves closer to me and I glance at Malcolm. He's scowling, but knows I don't want him to say anything. He pulls a cigarette out of his pack and lights it up.

"Not in the house, Malcolm," I say and move away from Dean again, feeling incredibly uncomfortable.

I know I need to do something soon. I'm going to have to tell Dean that I'm not interested, that I actually prefer his cousin to him. I've given him all the signals of my disinterest but he's not taking the hint, and sooner or later Malcolm isn't going to stand for Dean's pushiness toward me. Malcolm and I sort of happened in week one. It went very quickly from flirtatious glances to kissing in the dark when Dean was sleeping. I can't say that it's serious, but I like him and he likes me. But more than anything, I need him—I need his protection, from the zombies and from Dean's advances.

I clear my throat and search out a pan, putting it on the stove, and set to opening up the soup. I look out the window and see a zombie coming up the road. It staggers aimlessly from side to side, its gaze at its feet, its shoulders slumped. Its clothes are torn and filthy like a homeless person's, and I feel a pang of sadness for what this thing once was. A human. A father, more than likely, looking at his age. I wonder if his family made it out alive or if they are dead too.

I look away from the abomination, not bearing to look at it anymore. "Shit, there's another one." I point toward the unhuman thing shambling toward the house. "This one looks pretty bad." I say, looking back at it as it stumbles at the side of the road, falling to its knees with a sickening thud.

"I'm on it," Malcolm says and I hear his boots stomp off down the hallway. The front door opens and closes, and the sound of Malcolm's heavy steps descend down the porch steps. I watch the thing for a minute or so struggling to stand back up. It's back on its feet just in time for Malcolm to reach it and swing a large metal pole, hitting it across its skull. I bite down on my lip and look away with a grimace.

"You okay?" Dean asks, placing a hand on my shoulder.

I jump from his touch, and then laugh softly to hide my nervousness. "Yes, fine. Just this whole apocalypse thing has me on edge."

I feel his body heat close behind me, and fight the urge to shudder from his closeness. One hand touches my waist, and his mouth is next to my ear.

"You don't have anything to worry about with me here." His breath sends shivers down my spine.

"I know that, silly." I laugh, not wanting to turn around.

"You know I'll protect you," he says huskily.

"I do. Both you and Malcolm are great." I clear my throat, and watch as Malcolm rounds the side of the house and heads toward the zombie.

Dean's grip tightens on my waist. "Yes, but he'll just use you. I know how to treat a woman like you. I'll protect you

135

from everything and everyone." He spins me around to face him, his body inches from mine. "I've seen the way he looks at you, Anne. I can tell him to back off."

I force out a dry laugh. "Don't be silly, it's fine. There's no harm." My back is forced up against the stove, and I try to squeeze past him, but he keeps me in place with his grip at my waist.

He stares into my face, his eyes burning holes into mine, and I have the urge to throw up in my mouth when it finally dawns on me that he knows. He knows that there is something going on between me and Malcolm, he just isn't saying anything yet.

He smiles and takes a step back from me but continues to stare. "Well, if you're sure."

I scramble out from my position and reach for the can opener. "Of course I'm sure." I force my hand to stay steady as I open the can and pour the soup into the pan. My fingers fiddle with the ignition on the stove, but they're shaking too much to light it.

Dean steps up close behind me again. "Here, let me."

I move out of the way and let him light it for me. It doesn't work off the mains, but tanks that his grandpa used, and I know there isn't much left of them. Soon we're going to have to go old school and start cooking on fire pits outside— yet another thing I don't know how to do. Dean stands back proudly, a small flame glowing underneath the pan of soup.

"There you go." He smiles at me and steps further back so I can stir it.

"Thanks." I look out the window as I stir, watching as Malcolm drags the zombie by its ankles to the pit where they burn the bodies. "Think he might need some help," I say to Dean, needing the space from him.

"Sure. I'll go help him," he says, punctuating the word *him*, and walks away.

My stomach flips at the sound of his retreating footsteps and I take a deep breath, tears building in my eyes. He's getting worse, I realize. I know I'm going to have to say something soon. I can't go on like this.

Seven.

"Happy birthday to you, happy birthday to you, happy birthday to A-nne, happy birthday to you!" the boys sing for me, and I laugh and blow out the candle stuck in the middle of the slab of Spam.

"Did you make a wish?" Malcolm asks.

"I did," I say, my heated gaze meeting his with a smile.

I'm sixteen now. I never expected this to be my sixteenth birthday: trapped inside someone else's house while the zombie apocalypse exploded around the world. My parents were shitty, but I still believed that there would be cake, and presents, my first car. A party with pretty dresses, balloons, and dancing. I expected Steph to be there, and she'd more than likely slip vodka into the punch bowl. I expected my parents to briefly show up and act like they gave a damn for one day. I never expected this.

I burst out crying, and Dean scowls at Malcolm and orders him to move the stupid Spam cake away from me. Then his arms are around me as he holds me close. I cry more because of his closeness, because I want these arms to be Malcolm's or my dad's or Steph's—anyone's but Dean's. He kisses the top of my head and I cry harder.

"I told you this was a stupid idea," he hisses at Malcolm.

I force myself out of his grip. "No, no, it's fine, it's great. It just makes things seem so much more real, you know. It's just, this wasn't how I expected my sixteenth birthday to be." I look at them both. "I expected to be sharing it with my best friend, my family, and instead…" My words drown out

138

and they both nod in understanding. "I don't mean to sound ungrateful. I think it just got a little overwhelming."

I move toward the Spam cake and take the knife, cutting into it and carving it into three pieces. I place a piece on each plate and hand them to the boys with a smile and a sniffle. Malcolm takes it, eating the Spam in one mouthful. Dean takes a little longer, making sure to give extra time on giving Malcolm an evil look.

I can feel it in the air: things have shifted. Between me and Dean, me and Malcolm, and between Dean and Malcolm. As if me reaching sixteen has changed the whole dynamic of the group. Both men seem more possessive now, as if I'm a prize to be had. Their stares have become more focused on me and each other, as they both make it clear what they want. The whole thing makes me even more nervous, but there's no way out of this. I haven't left this house since this whole thing started. Three months we've been here. Food and water are running short now, gas is nearly non-existent, and winter is coming. I can't leave here if I want to survive, yet I'm deeply frightened at the thought of staying, too.

*

I clear up from the little birthday party, cleaning the plates as best I can by wiping them off with a slightly damp cloth. We can't afford to waste any water now, but we also don't want to let any food on plates and silverware rot and go bad. Dean says we need to start eating directly from the cans now so we don't have to worry about washing plates and things. Malcolm says we need to go on a supply run into town before winter really hits and we run out of everything. I agree with both boys. It's already getting cold, and we're already rationing food and water so much. At this rate we'll never make it through winter. We gave up a month or so ago on any help coming. There has been neither sight nor sound of the army or government coming to help in any way. Malcolm makes weekly trips to the outskirts of town to see if there's any change, to see if any help has arrived, but there never is.

As nighttime falls, I crawl into bed. We sleep in the little house under the house now; it's too dangerous to sleep above ground. One night we woke to find three zombies breaking through the windows to get in at us. So now the windows are boarded up and we stay downstairs. Each morning both boys go out and kill any zombies that have turned up in the night. We have our little routine now, and it works.

I hear Dean's breathing slow and gradually get louder before he begins to snore. I slide quietly out from under my covers. I creep past his bed and up the stairs, opening the door as soundlessly as possible. Malcolm is waiting for me in the living room, his body an outlined shadow in the dark. I move toward him, and his arms reach out to find me. They wrap around me immediately, his mouth finding mine instinctually.

He kisses me deeply, pulling me down onto the sofa with him, his hard body pressed against mine as his tongue invades my mouth. My hands cling to him, pulling at his clothes as his hands palm my breasts hungrily. We separate after a moment, both of us gasping for breath.

"Are you okay?" he whispers against my neck, invading the small space between my ear and throat with gentle kisses and making me sigh.

"Uh-huh," I murmur, my hands finding the soft skin underneath his T-shirt and running my nails up it. He hisses and moves back to my mouth, kissing me harder.

He stands up and pulls his T-shirt off, letting it fall to the side, and I do the same with mine. He lays me down on the sofa and climbs on top of me, kisses the small crevice between my breasts and then each peak as he frees my breasts from their bra. I gasp as he bites my nipple, and I grind my hips against him, wanting the friction of him. We've been waiting for this moment alone together for weeks, and I am completely ready for him.

"Are you sure?" he whispers against my mouth.

I pull away and stare into his face, only seeing the outline of his jaw and nose. "I am," I say with certainty.

And I am sure. So sure. I've wanted this since we first met, but wanted to wait—had to wait. I needed to keep one final promise to my parents. I promised them I'd keep my virginity until after I turned sixteen, and for some reason it's been important to me to do that. Malcolm doesn't need any more persuasion, and he stands and reaches down, pulling me up into his arms and carrying me out of the room and up the stairs. He takes me to one of the bedrooms and gently lays me on the bed.

His fingers quickly unbutton my jeans and slide them down my legs, stealing my panties at the same time. And then he does the same with his, and lets his boxers fall to his ankles. I gasp at the size of him. It's not that I've never seen a penis before—I have. I kept my virginity but not my virtue. But he's huge, and I shiver in both excitement and fear. He reaches down and gets something from his jeans, and I blush when I see him slide a condom down himself.

I'm so glad that I can see him up here, the light of the moon shining in through the window and giving more definition to his features and body.

"You sure?" he asks once more, looking nervously at me. He's been waiting for this for weeks too, and he's been patient enough to wait and not pressure me.

I smile up at him and nod. He climbs on top of me, pushing my legs apart and kisses me as he eases himself inside.

I gasp against his mouth at the slow intrusion of him as he eases into me and then back out. His kisses are heated and strong as he pushes his tongue inside my mouth and moves it against mine. My hands clasp at his back, digging my nails down it as his thrusts get less gentle and slow and become more forceful and urgent.

I wrap my legs around his waist as he speeds up. He presses one hand against the headboard of the bed to stop it from banging and waking up Dean. He pushes himself all the way inside of me and then pulls all the way back out before repeating the torturous pleasure once again. My body has adjusted to his size; the initial sting from his first intrusion is gone, and leaves me with a dull ache in my lower belly and heat blossoming down below. I bite down on my lip to stop the cry of pleasure escaping as his thrusts become more and more urgent, the quiet creak of the bed and low thump of it against the wall only urging us on quicker. He closes his eyes as he thrusts into me sharply and I let out a short cry of both pleasure and pain as he buries himself deep inside me before collapsing on top of me.

He breathes heavily against my neck and I pant as tingles continue to run over my body in rivers. He eventually looks down at me and smiles, pressing a kiss against my mouth again.

"You okay?" he asks between pants.

"Yeah, I think," I say, hissing when he pulls out of me. It stings and my body feels empty now that he's not inside me. "We need to tell him now."

Malcolm leans on his side, resting up on one elbow, and nods. "Yeah, I know. We'll do it tomorrow."

I bite down on my lip, both pleased to get it out of the way so I don't have to suffer Dean's advances any longer, and

Malcolm and I can be together, and nervous because I never know how Dean is going to react to anything.

I sit up and look around for my clothes. "I need to get back downstairs in case he wakes," I mumble and climb off the bed.

Malcolm stands up and fumbles around with the condom for a moment before searching for his own clothes. I slide my panties up my thighs, but when I tug them into place I realize how sore I am. I look at my fingers and see that they are dark with blood.

"Everything okay?" Malcolm says walking to the doorway.

"Yeah, just my virginity," I say, gesturing to the blood with embarrassment.

"Oh," he replies with a small grin.

We walk back down the stairs where we finish dressing, finding our T-shirts in a heap on the floor, and then I kiss him goodnight and slip back down the stairs and into bed. Dean isn't snoring anymore, but he doesn't make a sound as I enter and his breathing is still deep and labored.

I stare into the darkness around me, a chill of fear humming through my body but a smile on my face. How could I be smiling at a time like this? At the end of days when all I knew and loved was now zombie chow? I should feel bad. I should feel depressed or something, but I don't. Does that make me a bad person, I wonder, or is it all perfectly normal?

I ponder these thoughts as I fall asleep.

Eight.

I crouch down low below the kitchen window, the low *thump thump thump* on the boarded up windows and doors sending my heart into overdrive.

"There's so many of them," I whisper to Malcolm.

"How many?"

"Too many!" I yell-whisper back.

Dean scowls at me and I try to rein in my freaking out. He shuffles over to me, crouching close and then quickly stands to look out the window. The growls outside increase and he bobs back down and out of view again. The banging intensifies and he curses.

"She's right, there's way too many of them. We need to get down below and hope they get bored and leave."

"Bored?" Malcolm says incredulously.

"Distracted then, whatever. We need to get down below. Grab anything you think you might need, as long as you can get it easily, and let's go." Dean keeps low and moves around the kitchen, grabbing various things.

Malcolm catches my eye. "You okay?" he whispers, checking behind him that Dean isn't close enough to hear. I nod and he offers me a small smile.

We gather what we can from our crappy vantage point, moving around the house and keeping as quiet as possible. I go down into the underground house first while the boys continue to pass supplies down to me. I don't like the thought of staying down here, but right now we don't have a choice. It's the safest place for us to stay. There must be over fifty of the zombies out in the yard, and there's no way we can fight them off to clear them away. Dean was right in that we need to stay down here until they move on. Something will distract them sooner or later—if they don't get in first, anyway.

Malcolm and Dean come down the stairs, locking the metal door behind them, and then we're trapped. The silence descends around us—well, not silence, since we can still hear the incessant banging and moaning from the zombies outside, but trapped in this little underground house, the awkwardness between us three is evident.

"Are you okay, Anne?"

I look up sharply at Dean, his voice cutting the air like a hot knife through butter. His look is menacing and I immediately regret that we didn't try to make a run for it. I nod and look away, not being able to look him in the eye in case he sees through my lies.

"What about you, Malcolm?"

I look up through my lashes, my hair falling around my face. Dean is staring at Malcolm, who seems to be more than aware of the tone in Dean's voice.

"Sure, man. As good as can be expected." He shrugs and glances over to me.

"Should I fix us something to eat?" I ask, standing, needing something to do besides sit here and feel awkward and afraid. I go toward the little kitchen without waiting for a reply from either boy. I'm not even hungry, and when I get to the small space that is the makeshift kitchen I realize that I can't waste any of the food by making something to eat that no one wants. We have no idea how long we'll be down here. It could be an hour, it could be days. Either way, we need to ration.

I hear yelling coming from the other room, and rush back to see what's going on but immediately wish that I hadn't. Dean and Malcolm are fighting, and from the evil glare coming from Dean it can only mean that Malcolm has come clean about our relationship.

I stand in the doorway, not knowing how to stop them or what to say. It turns out I don't need to say or do anything as Malcolm's arm rears back and hits Dean in the face. The poor boy flies backwards through the air and lands on his back with a groan. Blood explodes from his nose and he passes out as his head hits the concrete floor.

"Dean!" I yell and run to him, crouching down to lift his head on to my knee. "Dean, wake up."

"Keep the noise down, they'll hear us," Malcolm says, coming back up to standing. He dusts himself off, gingerly touching his split lip. "He'll be fine," he says and sits down heavily on his bed.

"You don't know that," I hiss at him angrily, tapping the side of Dean's face to try and wake him up. "You could have killed him, you idiot." I glare at Malcolm. "Then we would be trapped down here with a zombie!" I add on to make him understand my frustration.

"I told you, he'll be fine. It's what boys do: we fight—or most boys do, unless you're this little nerd." He chuckles.

I stare at him incredulously. "Who are you?"

He rolls his eyes and scoffs at me. "Don't act so innocent. This is all your fault. You played us both against one another—you've done so for months now."

"What? I have done no such thing." I gape at him in horror.

"Sure you have. You wanted someone to keep you safe, and you played us both. Now I'm not complaining. I like you, and I'm glad that I won." He grins and heads to the kitchen.

I place Dean's head gently back on the ground and follow after Malcolm.

"What are you talking about? You won? Like, I'm some damn prize?" I yell at his back.

146

Malcolm turns to face me. "Please, don't flatter yourself. This wasn't even about you. It was about me and him, and him always thinking he was better than me. Well look who won this round, look who won the girl. Who's the loser now, huh?" He laughs and I clutch at my stomach in horror.

"I was a bet? To see if you could get something that he wanted? How could you do this? I thought you liked me." My voice hits a new level, going from angry to wailing within seconds.

"Keep your noise down, it wasn't a bet, not really. I do like you, but it was about proving to that little punk who's in charge around here. He's always thought he was better than me, put me down in front of our family. He was the brains and I was the thick brawn as far as he was concerned. Asshole had everyone believing the same thing too." He smirks at me. "Didn't see this one coming, did he? Who's the smart one now?"

I swing my arm back to slap him across his face, but Malcolm grabs my wrist and stops me. My body shakes with anger, and if looks could kill, he would be dead.

"I can't believe you would do this to me," I whisper instead. "You used me."

I burst out crying and run back into the other room. Dean is just waking up. He clutches his head and scrambles up to sit on his bed. He glares at me, his top lip rising in an angry snarl. I go to him, but he puts a hand up to stop me.

"Stay away from me," he says quietly.

"Dean, don't be like that. It's not what you think." Tears continue to pour down my cheeks and I wipe them away with the back of my hand. "I thought he liked me."

"*I* liked you," he says and looks away from me.

"I know, but I just didn't feel that way about you. I'm so sorry, Dean." I take a step toward him again, but he lies down on his bed facing away from me.

I go and sit on my own bed, staring around the room sadly. Malcolm comes back in eventually. He doesn't smile or speak to me. Instead he lies down on his bed and munches on a cereal bar.

The full force of the situation hits me then: Malcolm doesn't want me. Dean doesn't want me. I can't fight or survive on my own and winter is coming. What if they decide to kick me out? What if they use me as bait? The tears flow faster and harder, my sobbing getting louder.

What have I done? I think pitifully.

Nine.

No one speaks to me. No one helps me with anything. In fact, the boys don't even talk to each other anymore. Things are strained and stressful down here. And it smells, both from the makeshift toilet and body sweat. And we're running out of food, and since we're not talking no one is rationing anything—they certainly don't listen to me when I suggest that's what we should do. And we're running out of water. Things are screwed. Completely screwed.

The zombies got into the house at day two. We heard cracking as their angry rotten fists finally broke through the wood against one of the windows. Now their moaning and groaning is worse, louder and more insistent. They can't smell us down here because of the metal door, but they won't leave. Perhaps they can't get back out the way they came in, perhaps they know that we're here somewhere and they know they can wait us out. Who knows for sure? All I know is that if a miracle doesn't happen then we're going to starve to death down here.

As if on cue, my stomach growls loudly. I want to wait it out—wait for as long as possible before eating so we don't go through so much, but since no one else is doing that it seems pointless. Like wading against the incoming tide. I make my way to the little kitchen and root through some of the cupboards. They're almost empty, just some canned spinach and tuna. I try another cupboard and see packets of dry pasta, but we can't waste the water to cook it. I grab a handful and try and crunch my way through it but it's tough and hurts my teeth. I decide to suck on the bland pasta shells while I rummage some more. In the bottom cupboard there are several boxes of cereal, but when I peer inside, they're all empty.

149

I grab one of the cans of tuna and a fork and use a can opener to open it, and then slowly devour the flaky fish. It stinks up the kitchen and doesn't really fill the hole, but there's goodness in it—that much I'm certain of. A dizzy spell washes over me and I clutch the edge of the small sink to balance myself.

"Are you okay?" I flinch at the sound of Dean's voice. It's so cold and empty, and makes me want to cry that I disappointed him so much that he now feels nothing for me.

"Just a little dizzy, I'll be fine." I hold back the tears and take some steadying breaths.

I open my mouth to speak, but an explosion—so loud I worry my eardrums may perforate—fills the gap. Dean grabs me and pulls me to the floor, covering my body with his protectively. I scream out as another explosion rocks the house and dust particles fall all around us, pictures crashing to the floor. There are noises above us, things tipping over, ornaments smashing, and I swear I can feel my teeth chatter as another explosion rocks us again.

I can't contain the scream that escapes me, and I cling on to Dean as if my very life depended on him. Because, quite possibly, it does. But mainly because I miss the feel of other people, the touch and embrace of another human—someone to hold my hand, to stroke my back, and hold me when I'm frightened. Until this moment, possibly my very last moment alive, I didn't realize how freaking lonely I was.

Malcolm runs into the room. He sways from side to side and clutches a hand to his head, pulling it away to reveal a palm full of blood.

"Damn shelf fell down and hit me," he yells, and then nearly falls over as another bang rocks the house.

"What's happening?" I scream, clutching Dean tighter.

"I don't know, but I've got you, don't panic."

I feel his grip on me tighten and I burrow my face against his chest and continue to cry.

I'm not just crying in fear of what the hell is happening right now, but in happiness that someone actually still cares about me. That perhaps I'm not completely alone in this horrible world. Malcolm crouches down to our level, huddling closer to us. His proximity freaks me out, since it's the closest we've been since the night he took my virginity, and as he comes closer Dean must sense my unease.

He puts a hand on Malcolm's chest. "Back up."

Malcolm scowls at Dean and pushes his hand out of the way. "Pass me a damn kitchen towel for my head."

Dean does, and Malcolm takes the towel from him and backs away. He doesn't stand back up, though. Instead he leans with his back against one of the cupboards. The explosions have stopped, and the house has stopped shaking now. The zombies are a different story though. From the sounds they are making, they seem incensed by all the explosions.

"What do you think that was?" I whisper.

"My guess is the hydro plant. It was only going to be so long before something happened to it. Didn't think it would blow like this, but I guess it stands to reason. Which means we can expect the electricity to go off now. No water, no electricity, nothing," Dean says sounding worried.

"Shit's about to get real," Malcolm replies and leans his head back before closing his eyes.

Dean makes himself more comfortable and I curl up at his side, resting my head against his shoulder. I'm sure he's going to push me away from him soon, so I'll take what I can while I can. The zombies upstairs continue to growl and snarl. They sound so vicious and angry, and I dread to think what state they must be in now. It's been months and they're still going strong, not giving a damn about their decomposing sorry asses.

"I bet they smell real bad now," I mumble as the lights flicker on and off.

"Maybe. I mean, they will get to a point when they stop smelling. I guess they'll stop rotting, which means they'll stop smelling. Unless they are going to rot until there's nothing left of them?" Dean sighs heavily. "Winter will help a lot—the cold, I mean."

The lights go off and I flinch as we are swamped into darkness. Dean's hand goes to my hair and he strokes it gently, soothing my ragged nerves.

"I'm frightened," I whisper, not caring that I sound like a big baby for admitting it. Because I can't see how things can get any worse, and death seems imminent, so now seems as good a time as any to admit this one small thing. Because I am scared. More so, I'm petrified. I don't want to die. I don't want to be stuck in the middle of an apocalypse. I don't want zombies to have eaten my friends and family, and to be waiting upstairs to eat me. I don't want any of it. I begin to sob quietly in the dark and Dean continues to stroke my hair, and eventually I must drift off to sleep.

*

"I can't hear anything," Malcolm whispers down to us.

His ear is squashed to the door. It has been for twenty minutes now. The lights continue to flicker on and off every now and then, but more often than not, they are off. Regardless, the fact that they are on even for a moment is amazing.

"I'm opening the door," he says, holding the shotgun in front of him.

"Don't, please don't!" I yelp.

152

Dean's hand finds mine and he squeezes it. "Open it," he says to Malcolm.

Malcolm nods and unlocks the door. He takes a deep breath and eases the handle down slowly. I wince, though there is no creak or screech. No zombie dives to get inside, no screams of pain escape from Malcolm's lips. There's nothing. Yet nothing is actually just as frightening as something. At least something I can explain—at least partially. The sound of silence that greets us is a new fear altogether.

We head up the stairs, one at a time, but my hand doesn't leave Dean's. We exit our underground home and take a moment to look at the destruction around us. Everything is either covered in brownish blood or is broken. We listen for any noise, but are still greeted by only silence.

"What's going on?" I whisper.

Both boys turn to look at me, their eyes widening. I realize from their expressions that I obviously look like total shit, but they have no room to judge. They are both filthy and pale, with patchy beards on their chins and sunken eyes. Clearly they were starving as much as I was, and I honestly never realized vitamin D was so damn important until now.

Malcolm slowly makes his way to the front door, or what's left of it. Blood is smeared around the doorway, and I try not to touch it as we make our way outside. It's dazzlingly bright outside, and I put a hand up to shield my eyes. A storm is blowing hard, and snow has covered everything in sight. The only break from the constant white of snow is the smears of blood in it. It's pretty obvious which way the zombies went— their trail of destruction is evident. But what we don't know is why they left. And more importantly, if they're coming back.

Ten.

We walk as a triangle, with Malcolm leading the way and Dean and I following behind holding hands. We haven't spoken of what happened—none of us have. Some things are better left unsaid, certainly from my point of view.

The wind whips my hair around my face and the sleet stings my eyes. I tuck my chin down and trudge onward, not wanting to complain. The snow is crazy deep in parts, and we have to help each other to get through it. I hate having to touch Malcolm's hand, and I know I'm being stupid and childish but my pride won't let it go.

As we make it to town we stand open-mouthed in shock. Businesses have been burned to the ground, cars are crashed together in mangled heaps. I'm sure there are dead bodies somewhere beneath the heaped snow, and I'm glad I don't have to look at them. The most amazing thing, though, is that there are no zombies. Not a single one. I can't even hear their moaning in the distance.

"This is crazy," I mumble to myself as I continue to survey the scene.

"But where have they gone?" Malcolm says irritably. "I don't like it. Something has made them leave—either that or I've actually lost the plot." He keeps on walking and Dean and I follow.

Malcolm stops at a car and rummages around inside. He comes out empty-handed, kicks the tire and then continues walking. When he reaches another he looks inside and comes out with a grin and waves a pack of cigarettes. He takes one out and lights it and then keeps walking with more of a bounce in his step than previously. As I pass the car that he got the cigarettes from, I look inside and wish I hadn't. Inside is a body—or at least part of a body. The torn-up face stares out at me blankly, both eyeballs missing, the lower jaw hanging low and swinging in the wind. I choke on the vomit that builds at the back of my throat.

Dean squeezes my hand and pulls me onwards. "Come on," he mumbles.

We walk through the ghost town, checking businesses and supermarkets, house-lined streets and the little park I used to go to. But there's nothing barring dead bodies. We come up to our high school and my breath catches in my throat. We pass the main doors to the school, which swing on open and closed. The loud *clank* as they slam shut and then blow back open is unnerving.

"Should we go inside?" I ask.

It seems futile after everything we've seen so far today, but we need to get out of the cold for a little while and warm back up, maybe get something to eat. Night will be falling soon and we still don't have anywhere to hole up. The zombies could come back at any time; there's no saying that this small miracle is permanent.

The boys don't reply but we start to walk toward the doors anyway. Once inside and out of the freezing winds, things seem even quieter. The storm continues to howl outside, of course, but inside is like going back six months.

I close my eyes and take a deep breath, the scent of my school—my old life—filling me with such sorrowful loss that I nearly choke on the pain. Dean tugs at my hand and I open my eyes and keep on walking. The doors are open on most of the lockers, books, gym clothes, and other things in little piles along the hallway. We check some of the classrooms, but find nothing, and we're thankful, of course we are, but a part of me had still held out some hope for Steph. That maybe, just maybe, she made it through this. It was a stupid pipe dream though: the whole world was dead, apart from me and two boys.

We turn a corner and find ourselves standing outside the gym. Inside I can hear growling and my heart freezes mid-beat. All three of us look to each other, our faces paling, but we go on regardless, though our steps are now much slower. Malcolm looks through the small glass window in the door while Dean and I stand behind, glancing behind us every now and then uneasily.

Malcolm turns back to look at us, a small grin on his face. "This is messed up," he says and pushes through the door.

Dean and I follow behind him, preparing for the worst. However, the worst is nothing compared to what greets me on the inside. Two zombies dangle from their necks by the basketball hoops, one on either end of the court. Large stepladders lie at the feet of them both—knocked over, I presume.

I look up at a zombified Steph, clutching a hand over my mouth, and I sob loudly, my blood turning to ice in my veins. She kicks out and growls louder, the sound strangled because of the rope around her neck.

"I'm so sorry I didn't come back for you," I say, collapsing to my knees below her.

Dean puts a reassuring hand on my back and I cry louder.

Amy Bell gargles and growls loudly at the other end of the gym, her noises igniting some fight inside of me. This is her fault, not mine. Steph would have been with me if it wasn't for her. Maybe she would have died in the bus crash, maybe not, but at least she wouldn't have gone out like this.

I stand up sharply and snatch Dean's gun from him before he can stop me. I aim and shoot as I run toward the emaciated zombie version of Amy. I hit her shoulder, but the rest of the shots go wide, and by the time I'm underneath her, I'm out of bullets. She's going crazy, black gunk dripping from the one and only wound I caused. Malcolm aims and shoots her between the eyes and she finally stops moving. I turn to find Dean behind me, wrapping his arms around me. I sink into his warmth, losing myself to the months of pent-up pain and sadness.

*

We make it to the hydro plant two days later, after having to hole up at the school as the storm continued to rage around us. Snow was several inches deep, and many trees were brought down by the winds. I'm pretty sure it would have been all over the news if it weren't for the fact that everyone was dead—some pretty news reporter with red lips and bleached blond hair giving out the news that school was canceled for the day because of the storms, telling us not to travel in the unsafe weather, and to spend quality time at home with our loved ones.

But that isn't the case now.

As we reach the hillside opposite the hydro plant, we all stare silently at the mob of zombies surrounding the place. This was clearly what made those explosions the other night. Fresh snow has landed all around the plant, but even so the blackened and burnt earth beneath it can still be seen. Smoke still rises from some of the towers from a fire that no longer burns but is cooling down. The sound of the waterfall that runs the hydro plant can be heard in the background, as can a dull humming noise.

"What is that?" Malcolm says, his eyes straying to mine and Dean's hands clasped together. For a moment he has a look of longing, but then his lip curls in disgust and the look is gone.

Dean watches the zombies for a moment in silence before addressing us both. "I think the explosion has created some sort of frequency which is attracting the—sick. Look," he says pointing, and I do. I watch as some of the zombies push and shove each other to get closer. Small blue sparks crackle and hiss at their skin as they get too close to the wire fencing surrounding the main plant.

"So that's it? They're gone? We're safe now?" I say, smiling a genuine smile for the first time in months.

Malcolm cocks his shotgun and grins. "Let's blow these bastards away. Show 'em whose town this really is," he says, and runs off down the hill. He gets halfway and then slips to his ass and slides the rest of the way down.

Dean looks at me seriously. "What if they can be cured?"

"The dead people?"

"Yes. Those are our families and friends, that's our community down there. We can't just kill them. The government is going to fix this sooner or later, and then what? What happens when they come here and find everyone but us dead?" He turns back toward Malcolm. "We can't kill them."

"I don't think there is any helping them. Look at them, they're rotting away. Who would want to live like that even if they could be cured?" I say in total honesty.

Dean grabs my hand again and drags me with him down the hill, following after Malcolm. We slip and end up rolling the last part of it, collapsing in a heap together at the bottom, but Dean doesn't let me have any time to recover before he drags me back up to standing and we continue our chase after Malcolm.

We catch up just as Malcolm puts the first bullet into what was once an old man. The rotting body crumples to the snowy earth, black blood oozing out and splattering the perfect snow. Another zombie immediately fills the gap left by the old man.

Dean lets go of my hand and barges into Malcolm with his shoulder, knocking him off his feet. The zombies look at us, some beginning to shamble in our direction, and my fear spikes again.

"What are you doing?" Malcolm yells as he hits Dean in the face. His fist connects with Dean's nose and a loud thwacking sound can be heard. Dean continues to wrestle the shotgun away from Malcolm, kicking out at Malcolm's hand until a cracking sound can be heard and Malcolm screams loudly alerting even more of the dead to us. He finally lets go of the gun and Dean kicks it away from him and scrambles to his feet.

Malcolm continues to writhe on the ground, crying out, and I see the damage to his arm now, the odd angle it lies in. The zombies get so far and then stop, and I watch in amazement as they turn away from us and go back to the hydro plant. Malcolm climbs up to his knees, his tears mixing with his snot.

"You broke my damn arm. What is wrong with you, man?" He sobs louder.

Dean paces back and forth, his head clasped in his hands, murmuring something only intelligible to himself.

"There could be a cure," I say. "Dean said that they could get better, that the government could come and we could get in trouble."

"Don't be such a dumb little bitch, Anne. Those things are dead and ain't nobody coming back from dead." The irony of his words hits him and he laughs manically.

I turn away, not able to look at him or his damaged arm any longer.

"You better watch your back, girl. Dean is a loose screw. He'll kill you if you're not careful."

I look back to him and then to Dean, who has stopped walking now and is looking at us both.

"You don't know, do you? He's been obsessed with you for years. Little freak was stalking you before all this shit went down." Malcolm climbs up to his feet, grimacing as pain shoots through his arm. "Why do you think I was so intent on taking your virginity?" He laughs again and I look toward Dean. "It had to be you so I could hurt him, make him see who's the real man around here."

Dean looks broken, tears forming in his eyes as he shakes his head. "Shut up, Malcolm!" he yells.

"Is it true?" I ask him, my stomach hurting from the new knowledge.

"It wasn't like that. I…I just…I like you. I've always liked you. I just want to look after you." He looks shamefully away from me. "I love you, Anne. I'd do anything to protect you."

Malcolm laughs wickedly in the background, the incessant noise making me grind my teeth. "Couldn't close the deal though, could you?" He laughs again and I turn around to scowl at him.

"What did I ever do to you?" I hiss.

Malcolm grins. He reaches in his pocket and pulls out his cigarettes and awkwardly lights one before answering me. "I'm just the black sheep of the family, babe. I'm just fulfilling my job description. He can have you now." He takes a deep drag on his cigarette. "I don't mind him having my sloppy seconds." He laughs again, but stops as I pick up the shotgun from the floor and fire it directly at his chest without a second thought.

Blood colors the front of his chest, and the cigarette slips from between his lips. Malcolm clutches a hand to his chest, his mouth opening and closing as he sags back down to his knees and then falls sideways in the snow. His eyes stare up blankly at me as a final shuddering breath leaves him. Dean's hand touches my shoulder, and his other hand grips the shotgun and takes it from me. I turn to look at him.

"I'm so sorry. I don't know what came over me," I gasp.

Dean looks back toward Malcolm's body, raises the shotgun and fires at his head. It explodes, covering the ground with brain tissue and skull fragments and painting the pure snow a bright red. Dean turns back to me and drapes an arm across my shoulders. He turns me away from Malcolm's body and we slowly make our way back up the hill.

When we reach the top of the hill Dean looks at me, his mouth pulling up into a small smile. "I'll look after you, Anne. Always, I promise."

I look down at the hundreds of swarming zombies surrounding the hydro plant and then at the red splat in the snow from Malcolm's dead body. I look back at Dean, lean forward, and place my lips on his. He moans against my mouth, pulling me closer as his tongue pushes between my lips and he greedily kisses me back.

I pull away, feeling lightheaded. "I know you will," I say and take his hand in mine.

Odium III
The Dead Saga

OUT NOW!

ABOUT THE AUTHOR

Claire C. Riley is a USA Today and International bestselling author. She is also a bestselling British horror writer. Her work is best described as the modernization of classic, old-school horror. She fuses multi-genre elements to develop storylines that pay homage to cult classics while still feeling fresh and cutting edge. She writes characters that are realistic, and kills them without mercy. Claire lives in the United Kingdom with her husband, three daughters, and one scruffy dog.

Author of:

Odium The Dead Saga Series,

Odium Origins Series,

Limerence (The Obsession Series)

Twisted Magic Raven's Cove Series,

Thicker than Blood series,

& Shut Up & Kiss me,

Plus much more.

<u>Contact Links:</u>

www.clairecriley.com

www.facebook.com/ClaireCRileyAuthor

http://amzn.to/1GDpF3I

'She writes characters that are realistic and then kills them without mercy' – Eli Constant author of Z-Children, Dead Trees, Mastic and much more.

Made in United States
North Haven, CT
28 December 2023

46736494R00104